No Longer
Property of PPLD

out
with the
in crowd

D0354613

Books by Stephanie Morrill

THE REINVENTION OF SKYLAR HOYT

Me, Just Different

Out with the In Crowd

out
with the
in crowd

the reinvention of skylar hoyt

STEPHANIE MORRILL

Revell

a division of Baker Publishing Group
Grand Rapids, Michigan

© 2010 by Stephanie Morrill

Published by Revell
a division of Baker Publishing Group
P.O. Box 6287, Grand Rapids, MI 49516-6287
www.revellbooks.com

Printed in the United States of America

All rights reserved. No part of this publication may be reproduced, stored in a retrieval system, or transmitted in any form or by any means—for example, electronic, photocopy, recording—without the prior written permission of the publisher. The only exception is brief quotations in printed reviews.

Library of Congress Cataloging-in-Publication Data
Morrill, Stephanie.
        Out with the in crowd / Stephanie Morrill.
            p.   cm. — (The reinvention of Skylar Hoyt ; bk. 2)
        Summary: After turning her life over to God, high school senior Skylar feels torn between old and new friends, parents on the brink of divorce who are battling for her loyalty, and not knowing how to help her pregnant little sister.
        ISBN 978-0-8007-3390-2 (pbk.)
        [1. Family problems—Fiction. 2. Dating (Social customs)—Fiction. 3. Friendship—Fiction. 4. Sisters—Fiction. 5. Christian life—Fiction.] I. Title.
PZ7.M827215Ou 2010
[Fic]—dc22   2009032564

This book is a work of fiction. Names, characters, places, and incidents are the product of the author's imagination or are used fictitiously. Any resemblance to actual events, locales, or persons, living or dead, is coincidental.

10   11   12   13   14   15   16   7   6   5   4   3   2   1

For my parents,
Steve and Beth Hines
Thanks for never doubting.

All winter break, I'd planned for this moment, the one about to happen.

"Hey," Eli said as we passed each other in the hall.

I intended to say hello back, to smile like things between us hadn't changed, but something inside me bristled. I locked my jaw, turned away from his hypnotic smile, and picked up the pace.

Then I mentally kicked my butt as I sped toward my locker. That was *not* how it should've gone.

For starters, when I saw Eli for the first time this semester, I intended to be hanging off Connor's arm, transfixed by him and unaware of Eli's presence. Since Connor and I rode to school together, I assumed this would be easy to arrange. If only Connor hadn't questioned whether he'd locked his car, then abandoned me here in the hall to run and check, things might have gone as planned.

Secondly, I should've been casual and cool. A simple "Hey." A killer smile. But really, anything would've been better than avoiding eye contact and rushing off. Especially because I couldn't avoid Eli for long. We had first period together.

But deviating from the Eli plan did have its perks. It gave me something to focus on besides what possibly awaited me down the hall. When I chose my locker at the beginning of the year—seemingly a lifetime ago—it never occurred to me that my friends might no longer be my friends. That Jodi, Alexis, Lisa, Eli, and John would become the five people I wished most to avoid.

I took a deep breath as I turned the corner, then exhaled with relief. Just Lisa, who ignored me only when we were around the others.

"Hey," I said, same as I should've to Eli. "How was your Christmas?"

She shrugged. "Fine. You?"

I shrugged too. "Okay."

I'd spent my vacation days choosing between Connor's family—full of comfort and silliness—and mine. My moody little sister hardly strayed from the couch, and our parents tiptoed around each other, their sparse conversations sounding like two strangers chitchatting at a party. But at least we were all under the same roof.

Lisa shut her locker door. "How are you doing with . . . you know?"

Did she mean my parents' confusing separation, my little sister's pregnancy, or Eli and Jodi getting back together?

"I'm fine," I said, but I felt far from it.

"How's Abbie?"

"Fine." It seemed I should say something else. "We'll find out what the baby is on Friday."

"Cool." Lisa shifted her weight and tapped the toe of her adorable penny loafers. They had that "I might have borrowed these from my boyfriend" look, but with enough femininity to know they were chick shoes. I wanted a pair, something I'd never thought before about Lisa's shoes.

She noticed me looking and smiled. "Christmas gift. I never would've picked them out for myself, but I like 'em." She lowered her eyes, and I saw she wore false lashes. "They looked like something you'd wear."

"They're great." I tucked my bag over my arm and hesitated. I wanted to thank her for calling, for giving me a heads-up about Eli and Jodi, but couldn't think of how to say it.

Connor came around the corner before I figured it out. "Yep. I left my door unlocked." He glanced at Lisa. "Hey."

"Hey." She shifted her weight again and looked at me. With her cornflower eyes and those long lashes, she appeared wide-eyed and innocent. How deceptive appearances could be. "I should go. See you around."

We watched her stroll away. "It'll get better," Connor said, but what did he know? He'd moved every few years since kindergarten. He couldn't understand the difficulties of what I was doing, trying to change while everyone around me stayed the same.

Plus, it'd been like this since October. If things hadn't improved with my friends in the last two and a half months, what were the odds they ever would?

When Connor brushed my bangs from my face, I jumped. The gesture took me back to Eli, something that rarely happened when Connor and I were together. The two guys couldn't have been more different.

"Jumpy," he said.

"Sorry." I smiled, hoping to convince him that everything was fine, just fine. "I was thinking."

He slipped his fingers through mine as we headed down the hall toward our first class. "Can I guess what about?"

I smiled again. This always proved interesting. "Sure."

"Hmm. What would the beautiful Skylar Hoyt be thinking about this early in the morning?" He snapped his fingers. "I know. How you wish you could pull off my effortless style."

I gave him an exaggerated once-over. He looked the same as always—hoodie, track pants, and sneakers. "That's it," I said in a flat voice.

"I wish I could teach it, I do, but it's not really learnable." He shrugged. "You either have it or you don't."

I bit back a smile. "Well, I guess I'm out of luck."

"'Fraid so." He squeezed my hand. "So what were you really thinking about?"

"I saw Eli on the way in. He said hi, but I didn't answer."

"Why not?"

I shrugged. "Don't know. I guess I got so nervous about acting weird that I didn't know how to act normal."

"Or maybe you're more upset than you originally thought."

My laugh sounded contrived. "There's nothing to be upset about. Eli and I are broken up, and Jodi and I are . . . well, what do you say when you're no longer friends?"

"That you're no longer friends."

"Right. So there's no reason for me to be upset."

"That doesn't mean you aren't." He brought my hand to his mouth and kissed it. "It's fine if it's weird for you. It doesn't bother me."

"It's not weird." Maybe the more I said it, the truer it would feel. "I'm fine. Honest."

Connor paused outside our classroom door. "Then we're

going to walk in that room, you'll smile and say hi, and we'll go sit at another table."

"But we have to sit with Eli and John. Assigned seats, remember?"

Connor shook his head. "New semester, new seats. All you have to do is say hi, then follow me to our new place."

"You make it sound so easy."

"It's just saying hi. What's hard about that?"

The guy had a point. Surely I could put on a smile for my ex-boyfriend and say hi to him like I didn't care that he'd gotten back together with Jodi. Yeah, Lisa's call had caught me off guard. And maybe there'd been an initial sting, but what I felt now, this weird sensation in my chest, it wasn't jealousy. It was . . . adjustment. Not about Eli moving on, but about his choice in girls. Jodi had been my best friend since eighth grade up until last summer, when I got together with Eli and broke her rule about not dating a friend's ex. I didn't have the right to be weirded out by her dating Eli.

Eli and John sat at our old table, the one Connor and I had shared with them last semester. John's skinny arms waved as he told Eli a story, and I smiled. John looked the same whether relating an anecdote about standing in line at the movies or a near-death experience while white-water rafting.

Eli's eye caught on me as I stood in the doorway, and John's arms fell to his sides as he watched us. I hesitated only a moment before marching to the table. "Sorry. About earlier."

Eli shook his head. "No worries."

"I'm not sure why I did that."

He flashed his dimpled smile. "Because you're mad at me?"

"I'm not mad."

Instead of responding, he looked at Connor, who stood at my side. "Hey, man, how's it going?"

"No complaints." Connor reached out his hand, and the guys exchanged their usual elaborate handshake from their summer baseball team. He nodded at John. "What's up, Pratt?"

John grinned. "Just telling Eli about this wicked skiing up in Crested Butte."

Eli smiled at me. "And the tradition lives on—John rubbing his great vacations in our faces on the first day back at school."

"Like Skylar can complain," John said. "Her family always takes killer vacations. Where'd you guys go this Christmas? Costa Rica? The Alps?"

"We stayed home." Despite my best efforts, my voice sounded wooden. There hadn't been a trip this year because the planning got lost in the shuffle of my parents' marital counseling and Abbie's pregnancy. Instead, we sat around the house and pretended it felt normal to be home at Christmastime.

With his foot, Eli pushed out the chair across from him. "You wanna sit?"

Connor looked at me. We'd planned to sit at another table. To spend as little time as possible with the people who'd been my friends and now were so not. And sitting there then meant sitting there the rest of the year. Mr. Huntley, a former middle school teacher, firmly believed in juvenile practices like assigned seats. Even for high school seniors.

I knew all this and sat anyway. So much for all that planning.

Connor raised his eyebrows at me and took the remaining chair. I could guess what he thought. That this was a sign of weakness. That I'd never truly be able to separate myself. That if I couldn't stand strong on something simple like where we sat for American History, what chance did I have of resisting getting sucked back into their world?

I'd just have to prove him wrong.

❖

"Actually, I wasn't thinking any of those things."

"You weren't?"

"No." Connor hitched his bag higher on his shoulder. "You're seriously paranoid. I never said you should cut off your old friends. *You* chose that."

True. Although, really, they'd cut me off last semester and left me with little choice but to bow out as gracefully as possible. Though on the outside our group had appeared as tight a clique as ever, in truth I'd been backing out since Jodi's rager in July. That's when it became apparent to me that this path I was on—excessive drinking, flirting for sport—was potentially dangerous and I needed to get out before something bad happened. My decision to return to church, to pursue a life God would be proud of, didn't go over well with my party-all-the-time friends.

I groaned. "I just wish senior year was over."

"Hey." Connor stopped walking and faced me. "No doom and gloom. We're gonna have fun, okay?"

"'Kay."

He slugged my shoulder. "See ya around, Hoyt."

13

He took off down a branching hallway to his art class, and I continued toward English, smiling. Connor and I had started as friends. Well, *friends* wasn't the right word because he annoyed me, and Connor thought I was a spoiled brat. But Connor was the only one who had really supported my strides toward a life transformation, and that fused us. At first, dating felt awkward. We knew how to hang out and secretly pine for each other, but being a traditional couple—going on dates, saying "I love you"—felt foreign. Now, two and a half months later, we'd found a good mix of shoulder slugging and PDAs.

Inside the classroom, I spotted Jodi and Alexis huddled together, and the smile drained from my face. At one point in time, I'd have taken my rightful seat with them. But now I assumed they gossiped about me.

Funny, last semester I'd grown so accustomed to their snickers and snide remarks that I hardly noticed them anymore. My two-week break had apparently softened me. I wanted to hang my head and shuffle to a seat, but I mustered the energy to match them glare for glare and strut to the opposite side of the room.

"This seat free?" I asked Madison Embry.

Her dark eyes widened. We'd barely spoken to each other since sophomore year. "Yeah."

I glanced at Jodi and Alexis once more before sliding into the chair. Alexis's face burned red, and I could guess why. Several years ago, Madison caused the breakup of Alexis and her boyfriend, and my group never allowed her back in, never let her forget what she'd done. Though it was no longer *my* group, but Jodi's.

Madison followed my gaze. "Hmm."

"What?"

"Just noticing I'm no longer public enemy number one." She gave me a wry smile. "You must like him a lot."

"Who, Connor?" I asked. Madison nodded. "It's not entirely about that."

"He seems like a nice guy, but is he really worth losing all your friends?"

I glowered. "This is none of your business."

She held up her hands, surrendering. "*You* sat by *me*."

I turned away. I didn't need more enemies, I needed friends. I began the school year as the queen, the one everyone wanted to be, or at least be around. And now . . . well, now I was on the receiving end of friendship lectures.

"Hey," Madison said, her voice soft. "I heard about your sister. How's she doing?"

"Abbie's strong."

"I always liked Abbie. I mean, you could tell she might be trouble, but I liked her."

I didn't reply, just focused on writing my name, the class, and the date on the first sheet of my notebook. I'd committed to being a better student this semester, although I'd already damaged my chances of getting into a killer college. Luckily, I had no idea what I wanted to do with my life and was happy to spend a couple years at Johnson County Community College figuring it out.

Madison picked at her nail polish, same as she'd done years ago when uncomfortable. "Is she keeping the baby?"

"She doesn't know."

"Doesn't she need to decide that soon?"

The old me would've ordered her to shut her trap, but I didn't know how to nicely tell someone they were pushing my limits. Especially Madison, who not so long ago I might have called with intimate details.

She solved the problem for me. "Never mind." She waved me away with a hand. "We're not friends anymore. I'm being nosy."

Somehow, her saying this made me want to tell her, but I bit back the answer. Too many people had burned me recently. I'd lost interest in trusting anyone.

2

I cringed as I eavesdropped on Chris and Abbie's attempts at normal conversation. Polite exchanges about teachers and homework. Abbie's voice sounded tight—nerves?—as she shared a lunchroom anecdote. Made me miss the endless stream of flirtatious chatter they used to annoy me with.

The strain between our siblings didn't seem to affect Connor. He acted as playful as ever, tugging at my hair, calling me *mon cherie* in an over-the-top French accent. Though I often rolled my eyes at it, I normally enjoyed Connor's silliness, but with Abbie and Chris in the car, it seemed insensitive.

"Why so crabby?" Connor asked as he pulled down my street. Our tradition of carpooling to school began last semester, before he had a car. We'd intended to trade off driving responsibilities, but I rarely drove anymore.

"I'm not crabby."

"You are. Should we head to Sheridan's? Do a little custard therapy?"

"It's twenty degrees outside. I don't want to freeze while waiting for my ice cream."

"Bet the line would be short." Connor grinned at me.

When I responded with a bland smile, he gave an exaggerated sigh. "Okay, fine, I'll just take you home."

With the car idling in my driveway, Connor leaned across the console to kiss me good-bye. I pecked him on the lips, but he caught my arm before I unfastened my seat belt.

"Come on, that was horrible." He hovered nearby. I glanced in the backseat, where Chris brooded alone now that Abbie had shot out of the car. Connor laughed. "He's seen us kiss before."

He pulled me close for an admittedly much better kiss, then tousled my hair. "Scram, girl."

I laughed as I slipped out of the car. How'd he do that? In a matter of seconds, he could snap me from cranky to delighted.

"This sucks," Abbie said as Connor backed out of the driveway. "I thought spending a couple weeks apart from each other would make all this easier."

"Since when does time apart make anything easier?"

She rubbed her swollen stomach like she often did these days when fretting. "You should see Chris and Lance around each other. They both try helping me, and it turns into this weird competition. And you know how I feel about Chris, but it doesn't change that Lance is the father. He deserves to help if he wants." She sighed. She'd been doing a lot of that recently too. "I just don't know what the right thing is to do."

A big sister should have advice for her little sister. I longed to say something poignant to Abbie, something soothing.

I fumbled my key into the lock. "I'm sure you'll figure it out."

I cringed at my words. Almost anything would've been better than that careless statement. "That's not what I meant. I mean, I don't know what you should do either, but I'm sure you're handling it fine."

Abbie's gaze rested on my face, the lids of her cinnamon eyes heavy with fatigue. "Am I?"

I nodded. "Don't worry about the guys. That'll solve itself in time." I gestured to her belly. "Focus on what you want to do with this little guy or gal."

"Just four more days and we'll know."

"Hopefully," I said. Why did I always have to do that, throw in that negative spin?

"Yeah." Abbie looked at her stomach. "Hopefully."

"I'm sure the baby will cooperate this time."

On Friday, Abbie would have a sonogram that we hoped would reveal the gender of the baby. During her previous one, he or she had been sleeping and had no interest in moving. I'd kidded Abbie about the baby clearly being hers—stubborn. She'd burst into tears, and I felt like a horrible sister.

"If not, I guess you'll just be a surprise." Abbie gave her stomach a tender pat, and I wondered for the thousandth time if Abbie intended to keep the baby. Her official position was "undecided," but more and more she acted attached. And why shouldn't she be, especially now that the baby moved so much?

When I popped open the door, the scent of chocolate chip cookies greeted us.

"Man, that smells good." Abbie tossed her backpack to the foot of the staircase. "Did the guys accidentally drop us off at *their* house?"

"I heard that!" Mom called from the kitchen. "You really think Amy Ross is the only one who knows how to whip up a batch of cookies?"

"This I have to see for myself," I whispered to Abbie.

She grinned, and we traveled the short hallway to the kitchen. There we saw a spectacular sight—our mom sporting an apron and mitts as she pulled a sheet of cookies from the oven. A Viking, to be more specific. She insisted on buying it last fall, even though she never cooked anything more complicated than Stouffer's lasagna. But Mom always had a thing for owning the best of the best, necessary or not.

"You're making cookies," I said.

Mom beamed. "Yep."

"From scratch?" Abbie asked.

"Refrigerated cookie dough. It's still effort."

"It's great, Mom." I snatched a cooling cookie and took a bite. "They taste great."

And they did. That's not to say Amy Ross's didn't taste better, but I'd happily eat these forever if it meant having Mom at home.

Not too long ago, we often came home from school to find Mom either closed inside her room napping or absorbed in furniture catalogs as she planned elaborate redecorating. In October, when Abbie broke the news of her pregnancy, Mom left. We didn't hear from her for a month, and Abbie and I had both lost hope of Mom ever returning. But Dad kept calling her, kept leaving messages on her cell, until she randomly showed up at our weekly family counseling session.

Things between Mom and Dad still weren't great—Dad

spent his nights in the guest bedroom, and dinner conversation often felt forced—but at least there was hope.

Mom rested a hand on Abbie's shoulder. "How you feeling, honey?"

"Like I need a glass of milk." She shuffled past Mom to the refrigerator.

Mom gave me a quizzical look, but I shrugged. We'd all noticed how Abbie dodged pregnancy questions, but I didn't think we should push her yet. She'd be forced to deal with reality soon enough. March 10, if we could trust the due date.

Mom transferred the cookies to wire baking racks for cooling. "Your father called. They won a large bid today, and we thought we'd all go out tonight and celebrate. That okay with you girls, or do you have too much homework?"

Abbie dipped her cookie into the milk. "I'm never too busy for celebrating."

Mom glanced at me but looked away before asking, "Do you think Connor would want to come?"

"He's busy tonight, but thanks."

Okay, so that wasn't exactly true, but I dreaded being in the same room with my mom and Connor. She loved him, but she didn't like the idea of me dating anyone.

The house rule had always been no dating until we left for college, though it wasn't a rule Abbie and I ever followed—I'd dated Eli on the sly, and Abbie, well, she'd had her share of boyfriends. Connor and I happened around the time Mom pulled her disappearing act. When she moved back into the house, she tried breaking us up, but Dad overruled her, a first in my memory. Things were just plain awkward whenever Connor came over, so I mostly hung out at the Rosses'.

21

When we'd finished our cookies, Abbie and I headed upstairs, me to complete what little homework I had, and she to nap. I'd just cracked open *Wuthering Heights* when Abbie entered through our bathroom, already dressed in her pj's.

"You should ask Connor to come tonight. Mom needs to get used to the idea of you dating."

I looked at her. "You should figure out what to do about the baby."

Abbie's eyes narrowed. "Don't do that."

"Sorry. I thought this was one of those things where we give each other advice we don't want to hear." I turned back to my book. "This thing with Connor and Mom is none of your business."

"Don't you want them to get used to each other?"

"What does it matter? It's not like it'll be an issue much longer."

Abbie's eyes went wide, and she sank to my bed. "You think Mom's going to leave again?"

"No!" My voice came out high and squeaky. I steadied it. "No, I meant that I'll be starting college. Mom's not going anywhere."

Abbie still looked unsure. "You don't think so?"

I shook my head. "Abbie, she's downstairs baking. Dad comes home for dinner now. Life's back on track. It's good."

"Maybe too good."

Her words touched a nerve. I'd had the same thought at the first whiff of those chocolate chip cookies. Life was unsettlingly good.

"I think it's too good to last," Abbie said.

"You're being paranoid," I told her—and myself. "They hit a rough patch, but Mom and Dad love each other. They're working through it."

She pushed herself off the bed. "I hope you're right."

With that, she left my room. And left me nervous.

3

"You know, this used to be much cheaper for me," Connor said as he handed the cashier a ten-dollar bill.

"I offered to pay."

Connor became serious. "Never. When we're out, I pay for you."

"But I don't mind—"

"*I* mind. I don't know how it was with Eli, but I don't believe in letting girls pay."

An employee appeared at the window with our ice cream. "Caramel pretzel crunch." She smiled as she held out Connor's turtle sundae. "I wondered if I was making this for you."

Connor accepted his ice cream with a grin. "Thanks, Rachel."

The girl—Rachel, apparently—gave me a sheepish smile and disappeared from the window. She was cute, in a sweet and simple kind of way. I hated the jealous tickle in my chest, something I'd never experienced much before Connor. Of course, I'd never been in love before.

"I don't know how it was with Jodi either, but no flirting with other girls."

Connor fit his arm around my waist. "Boy, you're strict."

"So." I eyed Abbie and Chris perched on a concrete bench. They must've given up on making conversation, because they sat there as stony as their seat. "Do we join them?"

"Nah. They need some time alone." Connor guided me to the remaining bench. "Today's a hard day for Chris."

I shot him a sharp look. "It's hard for Abbie too."

"I'm not saying it isn't," Connor said, his voice careful. "But today the baby became more real to Chris. To Abbie, the baby's been real for a while."

I checked my cell phone for missed calls. None. "I still can't believe Mom and Dad missed the sonogram. That's so weird."

"You're sure they knew the time?"

"We talked about it at dinner last night." I held down the speed dial number for Dad's cell. "We told them the appointment was at 3:45, so you'd be taking us. Mom said to Dad, 'Don't you have a meeting at 3:30?' Dad said, 'No, I moved it for counseling,' and Mom said, 'Oh, I forgot about counseling.' So they decided to cut their session a few minutes short so they could make it on time."

Once again Dad's voice mail kicked in. I hung up before he could invite me to leave a message. I'd already left two.

"Voice mail again?" Connor asked.

I nodded. "I don't understand."

The back of my neck prickled with fear, or maybe just cold. Who ate ice cream when it was forty degrees outside, anyway? I pulled my jacket tight around me.

Connor's fingertips pressed into the back of my neck, warm from hot fudge. "I'm sure everything's fine."

25

I heard Abbie's voice in my head. *I think it's too good to last.* Those words had haunted me all week long, during family dinners full of elaborate foods our table had never seen—roasts, Cornish hens, salads with ingredients like feta and arugula. It *did* seem too good to last. It reminded me of other projects around the house that Mom dove into with enthusiasm—sewing curtains for the guest bedroom, an organic vegetable garden—only to abandon them shortly after starting. Was our family doomed to be one more discarded hobby?

"Why wasn't Lance there today?" Connor's voice sounded tight, like it often did when we discussed Lance. "You'd think he'd care."

"He does." I forced myself to take a bite of ice cream. Connor had bought it for me, after all. "His mom wouldn't let him come."

Connor's eyes widened. "Wouldn't *let* him?"

"They don't want him involved unless Abbie decides to keep the baby."

"How about teaching him to be responsible for his actions? Abbie has to deal with it regardless of what she does with the baby; shouldn't Lance?"

"I agree completely. Believe me, I wanted to call Mrs. Hartfield and say those exact things."

"But?"

"Abbie wants to handle it herself."

Connor absently tugged at his collar. "That's fine, but she can't let herself get pushed around by this family. All I'm saying is . . ."

But I didn't catch the rest. My eyes caught on a familiar black Land Rover rolling into the parking lot. While not an unusual car to see around this part of town, the flashes of blond hair in the driver and passenger seats confirmed my fears—Eli and Jodi.

I used to log all my time at Sheridan's Frozen Custard with Eli, Jodi, and the rest of our friends. All last summer we'd haunted this place, lounging on the grassy hill or secluding ourselves in the bed of John's truck.

"You're not listening to a word I'm saying." Connor sounded amused.

I nodded toward Eli and Jodi emerging from the car. "We've got company."

He glanced their direction. "Super," he said in a flat voice. "Although I have to admit, the week went better than I expected."

I thought of Jodi's frigid glare whenever our paths crossed. "I don't know."

"You gotta admit, it could've been worse. At least there wasn't any pig's blood."

My confusion must have been evident on my face.

"Like in *Carrie*," Connor said. I shook my head. "You've never seen *Carrie*? We have to watch it. How about—"

"Don't do it." Jodi loomed over us, wearing a sticky smile, the kind I assumed originated in the garden with the serpent. She helped herself to the empty spot on the other side of my boyfriend. "Really, Connor, do you subject all your girlfriends to that movie? Is it like a hazing of sorts?"

Connor smiled, a nice one, not a fake one. Connor didn't have a fake smile. "You liked it and you know it."

I'd had enough of this trip down memory lane. "You're not having ice cream?"

Jodi shook her head. "Coffee. Eli's getting it for me." She

stole one of Connor's maraschino cherries. "We're celebrating our last first week of high school. You guys too?"

Connor didn't seem to mind her thievery, just kept eating. "More like the thermometer finally cracking forty degrees."

Did he have to be so chatty with her? Talk about obnoxious. Had he forgotten what she'd done to me?

"You don't mind if we sit with you, right?" Jodi said. "I can't figure out why this place doesn't put in tables or something. Eli says they just don't want to encourage loitering, but we all hang out anyway, you know? Why not make it easier on us?"

Eli appeared, holding two steaming cups of something. "Here you go, babe."

Jodi looked up at him, her smile turning real. "You don't mind sitting with our exes, right?" She blew on her coffee and winked at Connor and me. "I figure we've all moved on, there's no reason why we can't hang out."

On the contrary, I could think of plenty of reasons, but I scooted to make room for Eli anyway.

Jodi cuddled against Eli. "We're partying at Alexis's tonight, if you guys wanna come."

"No thanks," I rushed to respond. With Connor's chumminess, he'd probably accept. He'd never had a drink in his life, but he believed in accepting people wherever, keggers included.

Eli nudged Jodi with his elbow. "Skylar doesn't party anymore, remember?"

"Silly me." Another toothy smile. "How could I have forgotten?"

Was she making fun of me? Jodi probably thought herself considerate doing so to my face. I'd rather she save her uglies for behind my back.

"Connor, Skylar, you guys ready?" Abbie called as she and Chris stood.

I bounced up. "Yep." I'd never loved my sister more.

"You look adorable, Abbie," Jodi said. "Really. I love that shirt."

Abbie smiled without revealing any teeth. "Thanks. My sister made it for me." She turned and ambled to the car, Chris beside her.

"See you guys on Monday," I said.

Jodi sipped at her coffee. "Come by Lexi's if you change your mind."

"I won't," I said, my voice flat.

Connor had to jog to catch up with me. "Do you have to act like that?"

"Like what?" I pitched my empty cup in the trash.

"Like you're better than them."

I winced. How easy it had been to slip back into it, treating others like they were beneath me. That feeling of superiority had the same cozy, comfy fit as my old Earl jeans. These new attitudes I was supposed to adopt as a Christian—humility, trust, joy—felt more like itchy wool tights.

But still. It irked me how friendly Jodi had been after a week of snubbing me. And how Connor let her get away with it.

"How should I have acted?" I asked. "Like you? Like everything was peachy?"

"Is this about her and Eli getting back together?" he asked, despite us rejoining Abbie and Chris at the car.

Concepts like putting on a smile and pretending things were fine—a way of life in the Hoyt household—were foreign to Connor. He didn't put on airs. He was the same at school and church, with our pastor and with his baseball team. I envied this, but right then, it annoyed me.

"You've been weird ever since Lisa called you about them getting back together," Connor said.

I felt my face flame, although with my Hawaiian heritage, only I knew Connor's words embarrassed me. "Are you implying I'm jealous?"

Abbie leapt to my defense, winning points with me yet again. "Skylar's not really the jealous type."

Connor looked from Abbie to me, amusement shining in his eyes. "I've seen it firsthand."

I chose to ignore the jealousy subject altogether. It didn't even deserve a response. "It's dangerous to be too friendly with Jodi."

Connor opened my door for me, as did Chris for Abbie. "Dangerous how?"

"It just is." I thought of Eli but didn't know how to explain. "You think she's just being friendly, but she's not. She's after you."

"Why? We've already dated."

Like I needed the reminder.

"I didn't say it was about *getting* you. It's about getting *to me*."

"You're being a little egotistical, Skylar."

Maybe so, but I didn't want to go through being cheated on ever again. I didn't want Jodi taking Connor away too.

"Enough fighting." Chris slammed Abbie's door, displaying a rare burst of impatience. "Let's just get out of here."

Connor sighed and closed my door, giving Abbie and me a brief moment of privacy while the boys circled to their side.

I crossed my arms over my chest. "I'm not crazy. She wants him."

"Connor's being an idiot," Abbie said. "I could see it from where I was sitting."

And that was all we had time for.

Connor started the engine and backed out of the parking spot. We waited for a break in traffic to turn onto 75th Street, and he reached for me. When he patted my leg, I met his gaze.

"Sorry," he mouthed.

I smiled and shrugged, feeling my muscles relax. Connor wasn't just my boyfriend, he was my best friend. That made it twice as bad when we fought because I had no one to call and gripe to. Except Abbie, but our closeness still felt fragile. Learning we could rely on each other was one nice by-product of her pregnancy. Which reminded me . . .

"Hey." I twisted in my seat to face her. "Did you get ahold of Mom or Dad?"

She shook her head. "I tried every number I could think of."

"Me too." I frowned. "Maybe counseling went long."

"I hope that's all it is." She rubbed her belly, frowning.

I offered Abbie what I hoped was a convincing smile. "I'm sure it's nothing."

When we pulled down our street, Connor spotted it first.

"Um . . ." He tapped my leg and pointed at my house.

"O God," I said, the only prayer I could eke out.

31

Abbie gasped.

Connor slowed the car to a crawl.

I couldn't tear my gaze from the yard. Dad stood amid the mess, bent over. He righted himself as we approached.

As we pulled into the driveway, I realized all the stuff belonged to Dad. His shirts, his shoes, everything from his side of the closet littered the lawn.

"I guess it didn't go well today," Connor said.

I gripped his hand. "I guess it didn't."

4

"Daddy, what happened?" I asked as Abbie and I ran toward him.

Dad waved at the guys as they pulled away from the house. "What time is it?"

"A little after five. What happened?" I stepped around a pile of white undershirts. "Did you guys fight or something?"

He looked past me, to Abbie. "I'm so sorry we weren't there, honey. How'd everything go?"

She tromped over the undershirts I'd so carefully avoided. "Fine. What happened?"

"The baby's healthy? You're healthy?"

Abbie crossed her arms over her chest and settled them on her belly. "Everyone's healthy. It's a girl. What happened?"

Amazing. For weeks, those questions had plagued all our minds—the baby's gender and health. Now, with our lawn full of dress shirts and loafers, they'd taken a backseat.

"A girl?" Dad beamed as he wrapped his arms around Abbie. "I can't wait to have a little girl around again. Congratulations, honey."

With all the activity, he'd apparently forgotten we might not be raising her.

Abbie pushed him away. "Why is all your stuff out here?"

"Oh, this." Dad surveyed the lawn. "This looks worse than it is."

As if we stood there discussing crabgrass or a busted sprinkler system.

I looked up into the bare branches of the sycamore. "Dad. Your *underwear* is hanging in the trees."

He followed my gaze and blinked at it. "Yeah . . ." But he didn't seem interested in filling us in on why.

"Did something happen at counseling?" Abbie sounded like a teacher trying to prompt a student for the correct answer.

"Nothing we can't overcome." Dad turned a big smile on us, the one I'd seen him use with clients at their annual Christmas party. "You know what we should do? Go to Ruth's Chris for dinner. It's been ages since we ate there." If possible, his smile grew bigger. "What do you say, girls? Get dressed up? Do a little shopping?"

"What for?" Abbie asked.

"To celebrate the baby, of course!" Dad's laugh sounded forced—har-har-har.

If I hadn't been so dumbfounded by his over-the-top gesture, I'd have grabbed his shoulders and shaken him until he fessed up. But why did his suggestion of a nice dinner and shopping surprise me? My parents had always used money to avoid problems, though usually it didn't feel so obvious. Standing in a pool of pleated slacks and tube socks made it clear the correct answer wasn't a nice steak and a new handbag.

"We could look for an outfit to bring her home in, if you like," Dad continued. "Your mom had the best time doing that for you girls."

He looked from one of us to the other, his smile still big and phony as he waited for a reaction.

"I'm gonna go lay down," Abbie said. She slinked away, a necktie caught on one of her dragging feet.

"Does 6:30 sound okay to you, honey?" Dad called after her.

She answered with a wave over her shoulder, then closed herself inside the house.

Dad gave me a questioning look. "She okay?"

"You and Mom missed her sonogram, then we come home to find the yard looking like your closet threw up on it. What do you think?"

Dad sighed and pulled his hands through his thick gray hair. "Will you help me clean this stuff up?"

Not long ago, I'd have expected this shifty, dodgy behavior from Dad. For most of my high school life, he'd been a mere shadow. Most nights he barely made it home for dinner, and even if he was home, I was often out with friends. He didn't get his act together until last fall when Mom left. That's when he'd invested himself in our lives, and we in his. Only to shut us out now.

But I couldn't just leave him out there alone with his underwear strung up in a tree.

I crouched and gathered an armful of clothes. "Where do you want this stuff?"

"I'm just putting it inside the door. Thanks, honey."

My knees cracked as I stood. "Where's Mom?"

"She's out." His voice sounded casual. Too casual.

"Will she be having dinner with us?"

"I wouldn't count on it."

So it seemed very little had changed in the last few

months. Mom and Abbie fled, Dad denied, and that stuck me with clean-up duty.

When I returned for more clothes, I found Dad on his cell phone, making dinner reservations.

"You might want to take it easy on the whole celebrating thing," I said when he'd hung up.

He stopped his sock collecting to look at me. "Skylar, I know your sister's situation is far from desirable, but we should make the most of it."

"It's not that. It's . . ." I hesitated. Did he seriously not know this? "Abbie might not keep the baby."

From the look on Dad's face, I'd guess that no, he didn't. "Why not?"

I heard myself laughing. Why was I laughing? This wasn't funny. "Because she's fifteen. Because things were over with Lance long before she even found out about the baby. Lots of reasons."

Dad's Adam's apple bobbed as he stared into the pile of socks he'd paired. "She'd really give it up? Give *her* up?"

My throat constricted. The idea of Abbie putting the baby up for adoption made me emotional too, but still I argued. "Keeping the baby closes so many doors for her. Abbie'd graduate high school with a two-year-old. *If* she graduated."

Dad muttered something unintelligible and returned to rolling socks.

"What happened with Mom?" I asked, fear stiffening my spine.

"Nothing you should concern yourself with, Skylar." His voice was silky smooth. "Everything will be fine."

I was coming to believe this less and less.

After dinner's stuffy atmosphere and stilted conversation, I headed to Connor's house. His nine-year-old brother, Cameron, flung open the front door and pointed a Nerf Blaster at me. He fired a round into my chest. "Gotcha!" Then he raced off, the dog chasing him.

Much better. I smiled and entered the house.

As I shrugged out of my coat, Amy came into the foyer, her fuzzy slippers whispering against the tile. "Cameron's hospitality needs some work."

"Clearly we're past the days of me intimidating him."

Initially, Cameron had had a crush on me and would bury himself in the couch pillows whenever I came over. That stopped even before I became Connor's girlfriend.

Amy glanced at my dress, black and strappy with a short, billowy skirt. "You look beautiful." Her eyes widened and her mouth formed an *O*. "Was there a dance tonight? Did my son make you go alone?"

I laughed. "No. Dad forced us into a celebration dinner. Abbie's having a girl."

Only after the words came out did I think enough to cringe. When Amy first met us, she'd said she would have named her daughter Abigail Amelia but wound up with four boys. Maybe it would sadden her to hear of Abbie having a girl.

Amy's face showed no hints of regret. Instead, she clapped her hands together. "A girl! How wonderful." She glanced at the staircase, I assumed because it led to Chris's bedroom. "How's Abbie doing?"

"I can't tell. She slept until we left for dinner and was

37

pretty quiet at the restaurant. But I don't know if it's because of the baby or because . . ." I didn't know how to explain because I didn't know what had happened. Dad remained tight-lipped about the events of their counseling session.

Amy rescued me. "Connor said it looked like your parents had a fight."

"To put it lightly." I lowered my gaze to the floor tiles, suddenly ashamed. "Dad's stuff was all over the lawn, and we still haven't heard from Mom."

Amy opened her mouth to reply, only to be interrupted by five-year-old Curtis. "Mom! Cameron's getting ice cream!"

"Excuse me," Amy said, rushing toward the kitchen. "Cameron Michael, what did I tell you about ice cream?"

As they hashed it out, I jogged upstairs. Chris's bedroom door was closed, but I found Connor's open. He sat at his old, scarred desk, chewing on the end of his pen as he read from his American History textbook.

"You're doing homework on a Friday night?"

Connor startled, then released the breath he'd sucked in. "Walk louder in the future." He swiveled his desk chair to face me. "And yes, I'm doing homework. My girlfriend had plans."

I sagged against the door frame. "She'd have rather been with you."

"Would she?"

"Yeah. She had a lousy night."

Connor cocked his head. "Let's stop talking about her in the third person."

"You started it." I settled onto the carpet, and he sank onto the floor beside me, touching his knee to mine. "My parents are fighting again."

"I assumed."

"Dad won't say what about, but it's gotta be something big." Emotion choked my voice. "Mom isn't answering her cell."

"It'll be okay." Connor smoothed my hair, and I remembered being a little girl, Daddy doing the same thing.

I squeezed my eyes shut and wished for those days, when we lived in the little blue house in a less fashionable area of town. Dad's construction company hadn't yet taken off, and Mom spent her days saving money rather than spending it. Did they fight back then? If they did, I couldn't remember.

The general chaos of downstairs reached our ears—Curtis's giggles and Connor's dad hollering at the dog, "Down! Cevin, down!"

Cevin's tags jingled as he trotted up the stairs. I adored Cevin, despite his stupid name. It was pronounced "Kevin," but the younger boys wanted to spell it with a C so he wouldn't feel left out.

"It's always so loud at your house." I nestled closer to Connor, wanting to bask in his warmth. "I love it."

Cevin burst into the room, bringing his big personality with him. With his perky ears and floppy tongue, he seemed to be saying, "Here I am!" like he just knew Connor and I had wondered.

Connor watched me rub Cevin's ears. "You need a dog."

"I'd love one, but my mom would have a fit. Can you imagine dog hair all over her white furniture?"

"I hate that furniture." Connor scratched Cevin under his chin. "I don't even feel like I can sit on it."

"It's nice furniture." Where did that come from, this sudden need to defend Mom's impractical decision?

Connor blinked at me. "I didn't say it wasn't nice."

Silence seized the room.

I looked away from him. What was going on with us? We'd had almost three great—dare I say perfect?—months, but now we suddenly bickered over nothing. I didn't want to add "boyfriend problems" to the ever-growing list of things currently wrong with my life.

Cevin's ears perked at something only he could hear, and he dashed out of the room, leaving Connor and me alone with this awkward silence.

I plucked white dog hairs off the skirt of my dress. "How's Chris doing?"

Connor shrugged. "He's been in his room since we got home. I went in there and tried to get him to talk about stuff, but he didn't seem interested."

Guilt gnawed at me, though it was a little difficult to pinpoint what I felt responsible for. Driving Abbie to Lance's over the summer? Being too self-involved to notice what my little sister was doing? "You think it'd help if I tried talking to him?"

Connor shrugged. "Go ahead." But I could see the skepticism in his face.

"I don't think I can fix it, but maybe he'll feel more comfortable opening up to me."

He frowned. "Chris and I talk about a lot of stuff."

"I know you do, I just . . ." And here it was again, my inability to communicate. Why did expressing myself feel like such a struggle these days? "I want to try."

He gestured to the wall his bedroom shared with Chris's. "Then try."

"That's all the encouragement I get? I'd find it adorable if you wanted to talk to Abbie about all this."

Connor batted his long eyelashes. "Don't you always find me adorable?"

I didn't want to smile—I wanted to hang on to my frustration—but couldn't keep the corners of my mouth from popping up.

The ice between us thawed, and Connor reached for my hand. "It's sweet that you want to talk to Chris. Just don't get your hopes up. He's not real chatty even under normal circumstances."

"You forget," I said with a coy smile, "that I'm an expert at chatting up guys."

I meant it to be flip, flirtatious, but I could tell it didn't resonate well with Connor. "I try to not think about that," he said.

"I was just joking." My heart hammered—why had I even made reference to my past? "I didn't really mean—"

"Skylar." Connor cupped my face and smacked a loud kiss on my forehead. "Go talk to my brother."

"But—"

"Now." He smiled (did it really look strained, or did I imagine it?) and gave me a good-natured push. "Go impart your wisdom."

Doubt wiggled around in my brain as I knocked on Chris's door. What exactly did it mean, that sour expression on Connor's face when I'd alluded to the old Skylar? Sure, I'd partied hard in the past, but that was all forgotten and forgiven when I turned my life over to God. Although people, in my experience, didn't forgive and forget as quickly as he did.

"Come in," Chris said.

I'd been focused on Connor. Now what did I plan on saying to Chris?

I nudged open the door to find Chris sprawled across his bed, belly down. He didn't look at me, just kept reading his graphic novel.

"Hey."

Then he looked. "Oh, hi. I thought you were my mom."

"Nope. Just me." I glanced at his desk chair. "Mind if I sit down?"

He shrugged and I sat. I looked about. His room hadn't changed since my last time in there a couple months back—clean, organized. Maybe it seemed this way because I'd just come from Connor's dump of a room, but Chris's belongings appeared to be arranged purposefully. A few car posters were hung on the wall, but they'd been framed, not just tacked up with silly putty. The books on his shelf were alphabetized and placed so all the spines lined up in a perfect row. The pictures on his dresser—three of family, one of Abbie—were arranged at a slight angle, toward the door.

I studied the picture of Abbie as best I could from across the room. I didn't recognize it. Her hair was in braids and she wore a sleeveless shirt, so it must have been taken early in the fall. When I looked closer, I realized she had on *my* shirt. Okay, I did *not* remember loaning that to her.

"She gave that to me awhile ago, when we were dating." I looked at Chris and found him studying Abbie's picture as well. "I guess I should take it down now, but I just haven't."

"It's a good picture of her," I said.

Chris nodded and continued to stare at it.

It touched my heart seeing how he valued her. How he'd let my messy, outspoken sister invade his organized, quiet life.

Abbie had been pregnant the whole time Chris knew her. She liked him too much to date him, wanting to keep him at arm's length so he wouldn't get caught up in what was already a complicated situation. But Chris relentlessly pursued her. I thought he'd run for the hills when he learned her last boyfriend got her pregnant. Instead, he'd been desperate to help in any way she allowed. Chris was sweet. Naive, maybe, but sweet.

"So, did you want something, or . . . ?"

I'd been staring at him. How embarrassing. "Not really. I just wanted to see how you are."

He shrugged.

"Well, I wanted to say how much I appreciate the friend you are to Abbie. It means a lot to her. And to me."

Chris snorted and scooted to the edge of the bed. "I'm a horrible friend. I do stuff hoping it'll convince her to drop Lance."

"She's not dating Lance, you know."

"Doesn't matter." He crossed his long, lanky legs and watched his jiggling foot. "She told me I need to move on."

I grimaced at the pain in his voice. "She thinks it's what's best for you."

"That makes it even worse. Here she's putting my needs before hers, but I can't seem to stop wishing she'd change her mind." Chris raked his hands through his hair over and over, something I'd noticed Connor doing in

43

tight situations. "If only I could go back in time and fix things."

Guilt plagued me once again as I dwelt on those sweltering summer nights when I'd snuck Abbie to and from Lance's in exchange for gas money. If only I'd changed my ways sooner and been a better example for my sister. If only I'd told Mom and Dad about Lance. If only I'd refused to drive Abbie. "Me too."

"I can't believe I'm losing her to Lance Hartfield. That guy's a major tool."

"You're not going to lose her to Lance," I said. "Look at today. *You* were there for her. Where was Lance?"

"I know. And inside, I celebrated." He shook his head, looking disgusted. "Can you believe that?"

"Don't beat yourself up for being human."

Chris didn't answer, just watched his hyperactive foot. Then he turned back to his graphic novel. A not-so-subtle cue for me to leave.

The chair squeaked as I stood. "I'll get going."

"Later."

I closed the door behind me. In Connor's room, I found he'd returned to doing homework. He pushed aside his textbook as I entered. "How'd it go?"

I sank onto the bed, feeling suddenly defeated. "There's nothing I could do, really. I guess you were right."

"It was really nice of you." Connor turned in his chair to face me. He rested his hands on my knees.

"You know, I knew what was going on with Abbie and Lance, but I just ignored it." I built up speed with each word. "Like everything would be okay if I closed my eyes. Just like my dad is doing now with my mom, like he always does, and it never fixes anything, it just—"

44

"Hey, slow down." Connor pulled me against him as the tears I'd been holding back all evening finally broke through.

"I'm sorry I yelled at you earlier." I sniffled. "I got freaked out by the way Jodi acted at Sheridan's, but I know you're not Eli. I know you won't cheat."

Connor held me even tighter and smoothed my hair. "I've never understood this about girls. You start crying about one thing, and it somehow gets connected to everything else."

I pulled back and blinked at him. "Just say you forgive me."

His gaze never left mine. "Of course."

"I can't . . ." I fumbled with the words forming in my brain. "If something happened to you and me . . . I mean, if you broke up with me or something, I just—"

He leaned close and trapped my words with a kiss.

I wished it could be so simple, that his kiss could take away these thoughts steamrolling through my head—like how I'd entrusted too much of my heart to him. That I bet he'd be tough to get over. That maybe my life would be better, easier, if I went back to being cold, hard, don't-mess-with-me Skylar.

But as Connor pulled me closer, kissed me harder, I couldn't deny how head over heels I was for this guy. I couldn't back out now. I'd just have to hope he proved a worthy risk.

5

"Do you believe in something being too good to last?"

Heather raised her foot from the sewing machine's pedal and blinked at me. "Be more specific."

I took a deep breath. "Like, do you think God ever allows us to live peaceful existences, or does he shake things up the moment we get comfortable?"

The corners of Heather's mouth quirked. It usually bugged me when adults looked at me like that—as if my big questions were so amusing—but I'd been around Heather long enough to not be bothered. She often smiled like that when she recognized herself in me.

Sure enough . . .

"Sometimes it's eerie how similar we are." Heather flipped off the sewing machine and relaxed as much as the straight-backed chair would allow. In doing this, she abandoned her shirt collar midway, something she'd always warned me against. "It's a tough thing to answer, because I believe our lives are shaped by the choices we make. But even making right decisions all the time doesn't guarantee a pain-free life. We see that in Jesus." She shrugged. "I feel our lives are a mix of consequences and divine intervention. God's goal for us isn't that we feel happy and relaxed all the time. His priority is our character." Her eyes crinkled with her smile. "That wasn't a very good answer, was it?"

I tried smiling back, but my efforts fell flat.

"What's going on?" she asked.

I wound a strip of fabric around my finger as I contemplated this. Thirty minutes ago, it had been Heather's shirt collar, but now she'd ripped it out and replaced it. Even half-done and lifeless on the machine, the new collar gave the shirt a totally different look. It's what I loved about designing and sewing—the tangibility, the clear and immediate changes. If only my personal growth could be so easily measured.

"I think my mom has left my dad."

I didn't mean to whisper it. After all, we were the only people in Heather's tiny house. But the words carried a weight I didn't like, and I'd kept myself from saying them. I'd tried not to even think them—not when I helped Dad clean up the lawn, or as I lay awake listening for Mom to come home, or this morning when I continually called her cell phone.

"Why do you think that?" Heather asked.

I told her what Abbie and I had found when we came home the day before. "Dad won't say what happened, so I know it must be really, really bad."

Heather flipped on her machine and resumed sewing. The soothing hum filled the room. "I've been told marriage is difficult. Lots of people I know, wonderful people who are crazy about each other, hit rough patches and come out of them just fine."

I thought of Dad's underwear dangling from the sycamore. "I think it's more than a rough patch."

47

Heather frowned. "Like they'll consider splitting?"

I shrugged. "Back in second grade, my friend's parents got divorced. I asked Mom if she and Dad would ever divorce, and she told me no, because the Bible says you shouldn't." I wrapped Heather's old collar around my finger, then unwound it. "You know, my mom used to be in charge of everything at the church. She was always doing teas and brunches and fund-raisers."

Heather smiled. "I remember."

"She doesn't do that kind of stuff anymore."

"That doesn't mean she's going to leave your dad."

I drew my knees to my chest and wrapped my arms around them. "I know. But I liked who she was back then."

"It sounds like your mom is going through something difficult. It'll probably take her a little while to work through it." Heather snipped a string. "Unfortunately, parents are just people too. They make mistakes same as everybody else."

"I guess."

I watched as Heather continued working, then dropped my gaze to the red satin pooled at my feet. Every Saturday morning, I escaped here to Heather's house, and we sewed, drank frou-frou coffee I brought, and chatted about whatever occupied our minds. This whole week, I'd peeked into my sewing bag at the yards of red satin. I itched to create the beautiful prom dress I envisioned—strapless with an apron back and an A-line skirt.

I caressed the satin with my fingertips. When I'd arrived at Heather's this morning—hands occupied with Starbucks cups and the bag of red satin dangling from my crooked elbow—I'd been hit with a sudden case of nerves. What if I screwed it up? What if the dress I made turned out nothing like the gorgeous dress I saw in my head? What if the apron back looked stupid? What if I should do a straight skirt, or an empire waist, or—

"You know," Heather said, interrupting my thoughts, "youth group resumes this week. We'd love to have you."

I pretended to consider this. As much as I loved Heather, youth group just wasn't my thing. They made us play weird games, then split us into small groups to pray together. I didn't mind praying as much as the games. Call me crazy, but I didn't delight in humiliating myself on a weekly basis by playing softball with a balloon wedged between my knees.

"Would I have to play the games?" I asked.

Heather grinned. "Too cool for mummy relays?"

"Everyone above age five is too cool for mummy relays."

"Maybe a little silliness is just what you need. It's dangerous to take yourself too seriously." Heather made a final snip of a thread and whipped her newly collared shirt from the machine. "What do you think?"

"Wow." I marveled at the improvement. "You know, when you showed me that fabric I wasn't sure. But you were right. It looks so much better."

Heather admired her handiwork. "That's why I always say not to stop in the middle of a remodel. Those risky fabric choices sometimes look like big messes when you're piecing it all together, but they usually have the biggest payoff if you see it through."

I remembered last July, when I came to in Eli's car after

that horrid party. I never again wanted to wake up hung over and blurry about the previous night's events. That's when I'd decided to make a life change. I thought it would be simple—give up smoking and partying, maybe pop into an occasional church service. I'd been ignorant to think I could do it apart from God, that my plans were somehow superior to his. And it would be stupid to think I could quit midstream. My only shot at happiness was to hold on tight, dive in, and anticipate the payoff.

"Maybe I'll stop by on Tuesday. Check things out," I said.

Heather shrugged. "Suit yourself." But I could see in her smile how pleased she was.

Seeing Jodi at church Sunday morning made my stomach knot.

Horrible, right? You're supposed to be happy to see people at church, especially people who'd never been there, but I couldn't shake the feeling that I wanted her to go away.

Jodi had dressed in what I assumed she saw as "church clothes." Textured tights, a pencil skirt hitting just below her knee, and a cardigan. She sat with Eli's family, her legs crossed and her gaze locked on Pastor Dave. She appeared wholesome. A girl you'd cherry-pick to date your son.

Jodi glanced my way and offered a slight smile. I acknowledged her, then returned my attention to the front of the auditorium. And straightened my sweater so the neckline didn't hang so low.

I intended to steer clear of her and Eli, but unfortunately, Connor didn't. We'd barely been dismissed when he grabbed my hand, said "Come on," and dragged me to the back where Jodi and Eli perused the doughnut selection.

". . . Tuesday nights," Eli was saying as we came into earshot.

"Hey, guys." Connor passed me a doughnut, one of the sprinkled ones he knew I liked.

Jodi's face lit up. "Hey!" She threw her arms around Connor in an exuberant hug.

I believe my exact thought was—*?!?!?!?!*

Eli didn't seem bothered by Jodi's too-friendly greeting or her sudden need to touch my boyfriend. Instead his mouth crooked in a half-smile and he nodded, as if I was a mere acquaintance. Ugh.

Jodi attacked me next, nearly giving me whiplash as she yanked me into a hug. She squeezed my neck like a boa constrictor. "Wasn't service great?" She released me and tucked imaginary strands of hair behind her ears. "I really like your pastor. He's so funny."

Connor's head bobbed in agreement. "Yeah, Dave's the best."

"My parents' church is so stuffy I, like, can't even breathe. But this is great." She licked icing from her fingers and smiled at me. "No wonder you wanted to come back to church."

How should I respond to that? It should make me happy to hear both Jodi's acceptance of my life change and her apparent interest in the church. But it took remembering all my mom's lectures on social graces for me to squeak out, "Yeah."

Eli crammed the rest of his doughnut in his mouth. Charming. "I was just telling Jodi about youth group."

"I thought it sounded sorta fun," Jodi said.

"I told her it's lame." Eli winked at me.

Connor rolled his eyes. "Don't listen to Eli and Skylar about youth group. They're such snobs."

"You like it?" Jodi asked. She looked at Connor through lowered lashes, and I thought I might explode. How dare she steal a flirting move of mine, especially to use on *my* boyfriend. Right in front of me. In church!

Connor, oblivious as always, flashed her a chummy grin. "It's great. You should come."

Jodi giggled and smiled at her shoes—horrible navy flats she should be embarrassed to own, much less wear.

Dad and Abbie loitered at the front door. He looked antsy, and she, sulky.

I took a step away from the group. "I gotta go."

Connor looked beyond me, to Dad and Abbie. "Yeah, looks like a good idea."

"See you guys tomorrow."

They all smiled and told me good-bye, then returned to their conversation.

I had a nasty feeling in my stomach as I walked toward the exit. Connor always kissed me good-bye, even at church. All it took for him to forget was Jodi batting her lashes and dropping hints at being interested in youth group.

What might happen if she upped the ante?

6

I planned to work on my prom dress after we got home from church. Instead, I stared at the red satin stretched across my bed. Did I really want red? Maybe I should go with a more muted color—black or eggplant. But I'd been dressing to capture attention since age two.

I rubbed the fabric between my fingers. Maybe the red was fine, but I should use a different fabric. Not that it really mattered. My date would likely wear sneakers.

This wasn't like me, this constant second-guessing. No matter what had happened in my life, I'd remained 100 percent confident when it came to clothes.

My cell phone hollered at me from the bottom of my purse. I dug for it. Normally Connor called right after church. It had been a few hours already.

I gulped at the caller ID display. Mom.

My hand shook as I brought the phone to my ear. How would Mom sound? Like a pathetic, sobbing mess? Snappish and mean?

"Hi, Skylar, how are you?"

Calm with a touch of chill, like she'd always taught me.

I swallowed. "How are *you*?"

"I'd like to meet for coffee. I have something . . . something I'd like to discuss. Can you meet me now?"

I glanced at the clock, a habit left over from the days when I had a social life. I rarely had plans anymore. "Where do you wanna meet?"

"The Starbucks on Nichols, okay? And if you don't mind . . ." She seemed unsure how to say it. "Please don't speak of this to your father or sister."

My throat constricted. I tried to sound normal as I said, "I'll leave as soon as I can."

I pulled the phone away from my ear and held it in my lap. I watched the screen flash CALL ENDED until it went idle and cooled in my palm.

I needed to put on my shoes and scarf. I needed to come up with a story to tell my dad. Right then, all the little details involved in leaving overwhelmed me, and I couldn't move. Especially because doing those things only brought me closer to the Starbucks on Nichols Road, where Mom waited to break the bad news—divorce. Or she might say separation, but we all knew where that led.

"Skylar?"

I jumped at the sound of Dad's voice. "You scared me."

"Sorry." He offered an apologetic smile from my doorway.

I noticed his coat and hat. "Are you going somewhere?"

"Into the office." He shrugged as if this wasn't a big deal, him headed into work on a Sunday. Not long ago, it might have been normal. But recently, Dad rarely brought work home, much less ventured to the office on weekends. "We're putting in a bid on a renovation downtown. I want to get a head start."

"Okay, well . . ." No reason to lie when I didn't have to, right? "Have fun. Or whatever."

"I'll be home in time for dinner." He crossed the room and dropped a kiss on top of my head. "See you then, sweetie."

I waited until I heard the garage door open and close before searching out Abbie.

She'd parked herself in the kitchen, in front of the family computer.

"Hey, I'm gonna take off for a bit. Are you—" I noticed the website. "Are you giving the baby up?"

Abbie turned to me, her face void of emotion. "You knew I was considering it."

Mom would've been proud of her polite, emotionless tone.

"I know, I just . . ." What? Why could I never turn thoughts into sentences at moments like this, moments when it mattered?

"Look at our family, Skylar." Abbie's eyes shimmered with tears. "The last thing it needs is a baby. When Mom and Dad were working through their problems, I thought . . ." She shook her head, sending her auburn ponytail swinging. "But she shouldn't be raised in something like this. There are lots of nice families who'd want her."

I leaned against the cool countertop, my heart heavy. I'd never been one of those girls who fussed over babies or jumped at the chance to be with kids. My disappointment caught me off guard. I'd wanted Abbie to keep the baby. I'd wanted to know my niece.

The words came out of nowhere: "God gave her to *you*." I didn't plan them or think them through, they just popped out. For once.

"That doesn't mean she's meant to be mine." Abbie stroked her rounded belly. "Maybe this is the best parenting I could do—keep her from being raised in this house."

"I . . ." I glanced at the clock. I should've been at Starbucks fifteen minutes ago. Mom would kill me. "I'm so sorry, but I *have* to go."

"It's fine." Abbie waved me away with a slightly swollen hand. "I'll be here when you get back."

I almost told her I was on my way out to meet Mom, but then I saw that look in her eyes. Abbie looked burdened, defeated. I'd keep her out of this business with Mom for as long as I could.

Mom, as expected, already occupied a table when I arrived.

She looked beautiful, wearing her ebony hair loose and her makeup light. Lots of my friends had pretty mothers, but not quite like mine. Her Hawaiian roots made her exotic, especially here in the Midwest.

The corners of her mouth lifted as I approached, but her eyes remained untouched. "I ordered you coffee, but it's probably cool by now."

My mother—an artist of passive-aggressive.

"Abbie needed me." I fixed her with my most withering glare and took my seat. "It's a girl, by the way. If you care."

Mom sipped her caramel-colored coffee. "Maybe you should listen to the whole story before taking sides, hmm?"

"All I know is I'm getting a little tired of coming home

and you being gone." So yeah, I sounded like a total snot. I didn't care.

Her left eye twitched ever so slightly. If I didn't know to look for it, I probably wouldn't have noticed. Mine did the same thing, acting up whenever I felt stressed or tried restraining emotion. I used to think it meant I was destined to become like my mother as well as look like her. I'd been assured by Dad, Heather, and Connor that I could decide for myself.

"Do you remember when you were a little girl and I had that friend, Irene?"

It took me a moment to adjust to the subject change. "Irene. Sure. I remember Irene. You guys went shopping a lot."

"Well, window shopping. We didn't have much expendable income back then."

I took a miniscule sip of my coffee. I wanted to like it, but regular coffee kinda grossed me out. Even loaded with cream and sugar. "Do you ever think we were maybe better off back then?"

Mom clasped her hands together. Her nails sparkled in the dim light of the coffee house. Was that how she'd spent her time since Friday afternoon, getting manicured and massaged?

"Actually, I've wondered that pretty recently. When your father and I were apart last fall, I spent quite a bit of time thinking about those days in the little house. It's for sale, you know. I happened to drive by on the day they had it opened up." Mom released a wistful sigh. "It looked so much like I remembered. Even Abbie's and your little handprints on the back patio." She looked into her coffee cup. "It's why

I showed up at counseling that day. I stood in that house thinking about all the good times our family had. I thought maybe we could get back to the way it'd been."

Mom raised her face to me, and I saw tear tracks. It shocked me. When had my mother last cried?

"I tried, sweetie. I promise, I did."

My hand reached for hers. "What are you saying?"

She bit her lower lip, and I noticed her trembling chin. "I always wondered why Irene stopped returning my calls. She just faded away, and years later I heard she got married and moved to Pittsburgh." Tears rolled down her face. "She was my best friend, Skylar. She was my first friend on the mainland."

Her hands squeezed mine so tightly I thought her perfect nails might break my skin.

"I don't understand." But my voice wobbled. In a conversation about your parents' failing marriage, the former best friend could play only one role. Thankfully, the Starbucks crowd seemed too enthralled with their own lives to notice mine falling apart over here in the corner.

Mom took a deep breath. "I didn't tell you this before because I was embarrassed and wanted better for you and your sister, but you . . . you happened a little earlier than we planned."

I'd always been told I was a honeymoon baby born a couple weeks early. Even though I'd suspected for a few months now that this might be a lie, hearing it acknowledged still took my breath away. What else had they lied about?

She chewed on her lip until the trembling stopped. "Your father was dating Irene when we met. That's how I met him, actually. I'd always planned to graduate and get my career going before I got married, but then Paul and I started dating, and . . ." Mom shook her head. "Well, someday when you're in love, you'll understand how mucky your head can get."

Like I didn't understand already? My boyfriend considered jeans formal wear. If anybody knew about getting mucky in the head, I did.

"We'd only been together a few months when I found out about you." She offered me a wan smile. "Both of us were from good Christian homes. We couldn't stand the thought of aborting you, *or* of people finding out we'd been sleeping together. So we decided to elope and play it off as romance getting the best of us."

I forced another drink of my cold, nasty coffee just so I'd have something to do. Whenever anyone had commented on how short a time Mom and Dad had been married before I came along, Dad always ruffled my hair and said, "The perfect wedding present." It made me sick to think about it now.

Mom steamrolled ahead in her story, appearing unaware that I could use a couple minutes to process all this.

"Marriage was tough. Much tougher than I thought it'd be. We came from such different families. My parents never fought in front of me, and your grandma and grandpa say just about every thought that pops into their heads." She sighed. "I wasn't the easiest person to live with, I'll admit that. Life wasn't turning out how I dreamed it would, and even though I loved you . . ."

"It's okay," I said when she seemed too uncomfortable to complete her thought. "Babies look hard."

Mom's smile showed her relief. "Thank you for understanding that. Part of why I never told you was I didn't want you to blame yourself or feel unloved. But seemingly overnight I went from being a carefree college student—looking for jobs someplace exciting like Chicago or New York—to being a wife and mother trying to scrape up money to buy macaroni and cheese."

She slipped her hands out of mine and kneaded them together. I spotted her naked fingers. No anniversary or engagement rings. No wedding band.

I swallowed the lump in my throat. "Did Dad have an affair?"

She nodded, no longer looking collected and beautiful, but deflated.

"Irene?"

She nodded again. "It was years ago, but I can't imagine the pain being any worse if it'd been last week."

I tried to divide out my own emotions, to figure out what exactly I felt and thought about this, but I couldn't. How could I feel both furious with my father and hopeful that Mom would forgive him, would work past this?

"I knew I could be difficult," Mom whispered. I strained to hear. "But I thought he understood that I was just overwhelmed. I thought that despite the arguing, we were happy with the decisions we'd made to stay together, to create a home for you and ultimately Abbie." She bit her lip. "But he wasn't happy. He had regrets."

"But I don't think he does now. Not about you, anyway."

"Maybe not." She appeared to be regaining her composure.

60

"And it was a long time ago."

Lame. Sometimes I still ached inside when I thought of walking in on Eli and Jodi, of discovering he'd cheated. He hadn't even been my husband. And for most of our couple time, I didn't know if I even liked him.

I opened my mouth to correct myself, to say something that might sound more empathetic, but Mom apparently didn't need my words. She dabbed at her damp cheeks with a napkin. "You're right, it was." Her normal tone returned, the one that said she was perfectly fine. "And the important thing is that, looking back, I have very few regrets. Maybe if I'd been a little more involved in your and Abbie's lives, your sister wouldn't be in the condition she is. But all that will change now. I'm moving on."

The way she stated it with such pride, I clearly should've felt joyous over this announcement. Instead, a pit formed in my stomach. "As in divorce?"

A curt nod. "I can't stay in this marriage, and for that matter, I can't stay in this state a second longer. I'm ready for a change, for a new chapter in my life." She squared her shoulders and declared, "I'm moving back to Kauai."

"Moving back?" My brain seemed incapable of processing this. "What do you mean?"

She clasped her hands and rested them on the table, as if this was nothing more than a business discussion. "Moving back. I'm loading up my stuff, and I'm heading home to Kapaa. I've already talked to Grammy and Papa. They don't think I'll have any problems finding a small place to rent."

My head spun with all this information. While Dad sat around and waited for her, she'd been making plans? Placing phone calls?

"But what about Abbie?" I asked. "She's about to have the baby. She needs you."

"I want you girls to come with me." Mom leaned across the table and reclaimed my hands. "Don't you see what a wonderful chance this is? A chance to start over. We can all use that."

And I cringed because of how appealing it sounded.

7

I couldn't just pack up and leave for Hawaii with Mom. I had four months of school left, and Abbie had about eight weeks until the baby came. And Connor. He should get factored into the decision. Right? Or was it too early for that?

A red light stopped me. I leaned back in my seat and tried to breathe normally. A million thoughts burdened my mind—he'd cheated on her, she'd leave us, my family had never been happy. And the kicker—Abbie would give up the baby for sure once she found out.

I couldn't handle all this by myself. I needed to talk to Connor.

The car behind me honked. Apparently, I'd been sitting at a green light. Flustered, I released my clutch too fast and killed the car. The impatient driver behind me blasted his horn as he squealed his tires and swerved out of the lane. He flipped me the bird as he blew by. Thank you. Because *that's* what I needed on a day like today.

Once I got my car up and running, I realized I'd wanted to turn several streets back. Great. I looked for a place to turn around and called Connor's cell as I searched.

"Pick up, pick up, pick up," I said through gritted teeth.

Voice mail. Ugh.

I held down Connor's speed dial number over and over, greeted each time by his obnoxiously chipper, "You've reached Connor, and I'm clearly too busy to talk to you. Unless this is Skylar. If it's you, I'm just away from my phone."

After about ten times, I chucked my cell into the passenger's seat.

Traffic finally slowed enough that I felt comfortable turning. I pulled into what I thought was a street but instead turned out to be the baseball fields.

I lost my desire to go home. Instead I parked in the wide-open lot and got out of my car.

Tugging my hat over my ears, I wandered down the hard, dirt path to the barren and lifeless fields. How odd to be in the middle of the city yet so alone.

I pushed away thoughts of Mom and Dad, the baby, and Hawaii. Instead, I focused all my attention on Connor and last summer. When I reached the concrete slab in the middle of the park, I stopped to look around me. In the summer, this spot was a zoo, full of families headed to and from games and kids whining for concessions. Connor and I had met at this very spot. Eli had left me to guard his bat bag while he went to the bathroom, and Connor approached me. He wanted to introduce himself because Eli had offered him a ride home.

"Connor Ross. Nice to meet you," he said, just like his parents had taught him.

At the time, it hadn't seemed like a significant, life-altering moment. To think how different my life would've been if Connor's brothers hadn't been sick and left Connor without a car. And for it to happen on *that* day, that very strange day when I first felt God pull at my heart.

As I sank to a bleacher, Aaron's face swam before my eyes. How awful that for the rest of my life, he'd be a part of my testimony. The story couldn't be told without him. He was the catapult.

Aaron and I had some mutual friends, and I'd seen him at other parties over the summer. We didn't talk to each other until Jodi's in mid-July. Sure, I thought he was cute, but I had strict rules about not approaching guys—anyone worthy would come to me. And that night Aaron did.

Months later, the details still felt fuzzy. Not only did I drink more than normal that night—stupidly trying to impress Aaron, who was a year older than me—but Eli swore he saw Aaron slip something in my drink. If anyone had noticed, it would have been Eli. Though we'd been friends since freshman year when he dated Jodi, Eli had always wanted more. At times his attention had been downright suffocating, especially at parties when I tried talking to other guys. But that night, Eli's jealousy rescued me. Had he not followed Aaron and me upstairs . . . well, I didn't like dwelling on what might have happened in that bedroom.

The next morning, I came to in Eli's car with a killer headache and an awful taste in my mouth. He took me to breakfast, where I picked at my omelet while he filled me in on everything that had happened. And when he leaned in to kiss me, I didn't know how to hold my heart back from him anymore. I'd resisted all those years because I didn't want to hurt Jodi. But after Eli saved me that night, I couldn't say no to being his girlfriend.

And that was the day I met Connor. The day I had

flushed my cigarettes down the toilet, sworn off partying, and started dating my best friend's ex.

The cold of the bleacher seeped through my jeans, and I stood. Pacing around the baseball diamond, I tried Connor's cell again. This time he answered on the second ring.

"Hey, I'm glad you called back."

"You are?"

"Yeah. Guess who I just got off the phone with? Jodi."

The back of my neck tingled. "Oh yeah?"

"She called to ask me some questions about church. Isn't that great? I mean, it's at least a step. When we dated, I could never get her to talk about anything deep, and now . . ."

Connor's voice faded away as I pulled the phone from my ear. He continued yammering as I hung up on him.

❀

At home, Dad stood in the kitchen with a variety of take-out menus. "Hey, kiddo. What sounds good for dinner?"

I glanced at the sleeping computer, the dark living room. "Where's Abbie?"

"Resting, but don't worry about her. She said whatever we choose is fine." The corners of his mouth quirked in a smile. "Actually, she made kind of a scene about not caring so long as she didn't have to decide. You'd have enjoyed it."

"I doubt that," I muttered.

"What?"

"Nothing." I took a deep breath. "So Abbie's upstairs?"

"Mm-hmm. I thought it'd be nice if when she woke up, dinner was here." He grinned. "You know how she gets these days when she's hungry."

"I just had coffee with Mom."

The smile drained from Dad's face. "Oh . . ."

"I can't believe you did that to her. To us." My hands trembled with anger, with disgust.

Dad turned away from me, his fair skin burning crimson. "I know."

Seeing his stooped shoulders, his obvious shame, brought on a rush of tears. "I always thought you were crazy about Mom."

He looked back at me, his eyes brimming as well. "Of course I am, Skylar. And I was then too, I was just . . . frustrated. I don't know how to explain it to you—or if I even should—but as a man, when your wife is unhappy—"

"You cheat with her best friend?"

Dad clamped his mouth shut.

We stood there in silence as the remaining sunlight faded to gray.

"I could've kept it a secret," he said in a broken voice. He kept his gaze trained on the countertop. "I managed to do that all these years. But your mom and I have a chance for a fresh start, and I didn't want to hide it from her anymore."

"Even if it means losing her?"

He frowned. "Your mom's mad, but she'll come home."

I thought of Hawaii, of the determination in Mom's eyes. "Will she?"

"Your mom has always done what's best for this family." Dad's normal confident tone returned. "Even when it didn't exactly line up with her emotions."

But what if she thought the best thing was to end it?

8

When Connor pulled into the driveway to pick us up for school, Abbie had been awake only a few minutes. The challenge of coaxing her out of bed grew each morning.

As I jogged down the front path to meet him, Connor lowered his window.

"What's going on?" he asked, taking note of my socked feet and lack of backpack.

"We're running a little behind this morning." I shielded my eyes from the morning sun. "We'll drive separately, okay?"

Connor hesitated. "We can wait."

"No, go ahead. She just now got in the shower. It could be awhile."

Chris leaned forward from the backseat. "What's happening?"

"Abbie's kinda slow this morning. We're gonna drive ourselves."

Chris hiked a leg over the center console and wiggled his way to the front seat. As he settled in, Connor studied my face. "I tried calling you back last night. I never could get you."

"Yeah, sorry." I shrugged, hoping to look casual. "Just bad timing, I guess."

The way Connor looked at me, I could tell he knew something was up. He lowered his voice even more. "You know, I'm not interested in Jodi."

Okay, so he even knew *what* was up. Why should that surprise me? He'd always been able to pinpoint things about me—traits, feelings, circumstances—that even I couldn't put a finger on. His deep understanding of me had made me fall for him. Now it annoyed me.

I raised my eyebrows. "I never said you were."

Connor massaged the bridge of his nose. "Ice princess voice. Look, Skylar, what was I supposed to do? Hang up on her?"

"Of course not." I took a couple steps back. "See you guys at school."

With a wave, I turned and walked away, even though Connor's eyes begged me not to. What he didn't seem capable of understanding—okay, what I'd never really told him—was how eerily similar this whole situation with him and Jodi felt. It didn't matter if he denied interest in Jodi. Even if he felt it, would he really tell me? Eli had denied it. "That's crazy," he'd said when I suggested it. "You're just being paranoid."

Five minutes later, I'd caught them.

How could I trust Connor on this? Guys could be really stupid when it came to beautiful girls. And Connor didn't know Jodi like I did. He didn't know how she obsessed over, thirsted for, revenge. He didn't know I used to help her plan her assaults. Fine by me. Connor knew about a lot of my junk, witnessed some of it firsthand, but I told him things strictly on a need-to-know basis. Surely even he had limits on how much of my past he could overlook.

Abbie paused the blow-dryer when I returned to our bathroom. "Was Connor mad?"

"No, he was fine."

She sighed. "He's so nice."

Yes, he was. Maybe too nice.

*

During American History, I focused every mite of my attention on Mr. Huntley's lecture about the cotton gin. I never even glanced at Connor, though in my peripheral I often caught him watching me.

"Are you mad at me?" he murmured halfway into class.

"I'm focused," I said.

I didn't mean to be snotty, or an "ice princess," like he'd said. I just lacked the energy for dealing with him. I had a mom who wanted me to move with her to Hawaii, a dad who thought she'd still come home, and a sister deciding whether or not to keep my niece. That left very little time to obsess about who my boyfriend might be crushing on.

"So are we gonna talk or what?" Connor asked as I packed away my history textbook.

"There's nothing to talk about."

He sighed. "Don't do this."

"I'm not doing anything." I looked at Eli and John, who blatantly eavesdropped. They turned away at my glare.

Connor, of course, didn't allow them to inhibit him. "What happened to the girl who used to yell at me every two minutes? Who told me everything she felt? Everything she thought *I* should feel?"

I hitched my bag over my shoulder. "She sounds kind of obnoxious."

"I liked her." He brushed my chin with his fingertip, a strangely intimate gesture for him, especially at school. "Please. Let's just talk about this so we can move on."

I headed for the door, away from Eli and John. Connor fell into step with me. I weighed my options as we walked— if I didn't talk to him about this, it would fester and we'd break up. The results of talking about it couldn't be any worse than that, could they?

"Jodi just makes me nervous." I squeezed my binder against my chest, hoping to conceal my trembling hands. "I mean, I hope she's being sincere with all this church stuff, but I can't shake my fear that somehow this is all . . ."

"All what?"

"All some plan to get back at me."

Connor's forehead wrinkled. "Get back at you for what?"

"For dating you."

"But why would she care about me? She's dating Eli."

"It's complicated."

"Sounds like it." He laced his fingers through mine. "You know what I think?"

I cringed. "What?"

"Now, why would you make that face? Why do you assume what I'm going to say is bad?"

"Instinct."

He slowed to a stop as we reached our parting hallways. "All I was going to say is that I think you're being a little paranoid because of what happened with Jodi and Eli, but that's a totally different situation. Okay, why the sour face?"

"Do me a favor. Don't use the word *paranoid*."

He cocked his head. "Why not?"

"Just . . ." Nope. Not ready to talk to him about Eli. "Just don't."

"Whatever you want." He brought my hand to his mouth and brushed it with a light kiss. "See you in Pre-Cal."

When I entered English, I found Jodi and Alexis huddled together same as last week, only this time, Jodi grinned and waved. "You can sit with us if you want."

She appeared sincere. Alexis narrowed her eyes. Understandable. When I left the group, everybody bumped up one step, Jodi to my former spot as queen and Alexis into Jodi's role. So of course Alexis didn't want Jodi and me getting chummy again. It might mean a downgrade.

"It's okay." I plopped my stuff on the desk I'd used all last week.

I thought Jodi would let it drop, would return to her conversation with Alexis and accept that we'd parted ways. Instead she walked over to me. "Are you going to youth group tomorrow night?" Her fingernails danced on my desk, so I knew she felt nervous.

"I don't know." I pulled *Wuthering Heights* from my bag. "Why?"

"Eli said he doesn't want to go, and I'm afraid to go by myself." She shrugged. "I thought it'd be nice if you and Connor were there."

Seriously? She was inviting me to my own youth group event?

"I don't know what Connor told you, but I've been going to youth group." Okay, I couldn't stand to blatantly lie. "I mean, not always, but I plan to this semester."

"Great." Jodi turned her smile on Madison as she approached. "Hey, Madison. Great sweater."

Madison gave her a wary look. "Thanks."

"See you later." Jodi waved, then bounced back to a sulking Alexis.

"So, that was weird," Madison said as she took her seat.

So Madison could see it too! Victory surged through me. "I know, right? She's up to something. It's obvious."

She shrugged. "Or maybe Jodi's changing. After all, I never believed you would."

Madison had a point. I returned to my book, deflated.

"So your mom actually thinks there's a chance of you and Abbie packing up and moving? Maybe . . ." Connor paused for a breath. He opened his mouth, then shook his head and closed it. "Nope. Can't think of any way that could possibly make sense. She thinks you should finish school over there? That Abbie should find a new doctor?"

I shrugged and tipped back my water. "Guess so."

"That's crazy. You told her that, right?"

"Yeah." Hadn't I? It all seemed a little hazy after she dropped the Kauai bomb.

Connor grinned. "I wish I could've been there when you told Abbie. I bet she was furious."

"I didn't tell her." I stabbed at my salad. I didn't have to look at Connor to know this confused him. "Abbie's kinda . . . well, she's wrestling with some big stuff right now. It seemed insensitive to tell her about Mom."

I looked up and found him studying my face.

73

"What?" I asked.

"You're not . . ."

"I'm not what?"

He placed his sandwich on the tray and folded his arms on the table. "You're not thinking about going, are you?"

"Of course not! Start a new school second semester senior year? That sounds horrible. How can you think I'd do that? I mean, I'd never even consider it." I forced myself to clamp my jaw shut. How'd that Shakespearean thing go, about protesting too much? I might as well have waved a huge banner saying, *Part of me wants out of here!*

Connor shrugged. "You've been talking a lot about fresh starts and getting away from everything."

"I'm not going anywhere." But a sense of dread filled me. What if that was truer than I'd like it to be?

He picked up his sandwich. "I just wondered, is all. Thought your mom's offer might have been a little appealing."

I rolled a couple cherry tomatoes to the side of my plate, where I'd be sure not to eat them. It also kept me from having to look at Connor as I asked, "Would you miss me?"

"You kidding?" I peeked up in time to see his face bloom into a smile, slow and sweet. "I'm starting to wonder how I lived without you."

My stomach flip-flopped. All that awkwardness of the last week—prompted by my weird freak-out to the news of Eli and Jodi getting back together—melted away.

"I wonder how you did too," I said with a wink.

And we were back to being us. Skylar and Connor, so mismatched it somehow worked.

"You guys mind if we sit here?"

I looked up at the couple invading our moment. What can you say when there are five empty spaces at your table?

Even as I said, "Sure," Jodi and Eli had already claimed a couple chairs. I imagined they couldn't conceive of a Shawnee Mission High student who wouldn't welcome them at their lunch table. How embarrassing that I'd been like them not so long ago.

"I nearly fell asleep during English class. What about you, Skylar?" Jodi unscrewed the cap on her juice bottle. "*Wuthering Heights* is, like, so boring."

"You think anything that's not *People* magazine is boring," Eli said.

Jodi giggled and elbowed him in the ribs. "Shut up. I do not."

John took the seat next to Connor. Great. We had a full invasion on our hands. I inched closer to Connor.

"I hate that blonde cashier," John said, his tray clattering to the table. "She always gives me attitude."

"You think everyone gives you attitude," Jodi said.

"Well, she really does."

Eli nodded at Jodi. "She does. I've seen it firsthand."

I glanced at Connor and found him already looking at me, an amused smile tugging at the corners of his mouth. Beneath the table, he pressed his knee against mine. *We're in this together*, he seemed to say.

Alexis had already set her tray on the other side of John when she spotted me. "Oh." She blinked her heavily shadowed eyes. "Hi."

My smile might not have been friendly, but at least I smiled. "Hey."

She pressed her freshly painted lips into a line as she took a seat.

"Where's Lisa?" Jodi asked, pretending not to notice the tension between us.

Alexis made her characteristic *humph*. "Probably harassing one of the cafeteria workers about the lack of nonfat salad dressings."

Jodi and I weren't the only friends who'd broken up last semester. Alexis and Lisa used to be the perfect picture of bff, but all that changed when Alexis started dating John on the sly. Lisa and John had been together off and on since junior year.

Yes, the time had definitely come for us all to part ways. Our clique, formed freshman year, had become far too incestuous.

Jodi popped a potato chip into her mouth. "It's good to be health conscious. I probably should be."

I glanced at Eli, half hoping he wouldn't take the bait.

But Eli had perfected the art of being a boyfriend. Except when it came to lusting after his girlfriend's best friend. "What are you talking about?" He pinched Jodi's skinny side. "What you should do is go back for another bag of chips. You're *too* skinny."

Jodi flushed, clearly pleased.

"You're, like, the perfect size," Alexis added. Suck-up. "Lisa, on the other hand—"

"Oh, knock it off." John sounded disgusted. "There's nothing wrong with the way Lisa looks."

Alexis's lips puckered, but of course she'd invited the opportunity for John's comment.

Ah . . . how nice not to belong to this group, to no longer

base my self-worth on their opinions. Good thing too, because judging by Alexis's cold gaze, she didn't think much of me.

Lisa slid into the remaining seat beside me and smiled. "Well, look at this. We're all back together."

This earned me another glare from Alexis, though this one also seemed to be for Lisa.

Lisa didn't appear to notice. She'd probably gotten used to it by now. "So, I hate that blonde cashier."

John laughed. "She's horrible, isn't she?"

"I feel sorry for her," Lisa said, chomping into a carrot. "Putting out such a rotten vibe? She's gonna have horrible karma."

John responded with an enthusiastic nod.

Even with Alexis's rude behavior, I kinda felt sorry for her. Sure, she shouldn't have dated John in the first place, and yeah, she'd been giving me the evil eye ever since Jodi and I fell apart. But I knew how much it sucked to watch your boyfriend flirt with another girl. Even if he did it unintentionally.

Connor nudged me. "Jodi asked how Abbie's doing."

I glanced across the table and found a polite smile pasted on Jodi's face. "Sorry. She's doing fine."

"Connor said she's having a girl. Is she excited?"

I thought of Abbie scrolling through the adoption website. "It's hard to say."

"I bet you're glad you didn't plan on going away to college."

I shrugged. "I guess so."

Jodi took a dainty sip of her juice. "I'd want to stick around if I was about to have a niece. I love babies."

My throat constricted as I thought of Abbie handing her baby girl over to a strange, faceless couple. I didn't love babies, but oddly, I already loved *this* one.

But of course it was easy for me to want to keep the baby, wasn't it? It wouldn't be me pouring out my life. Abbie would be the one making the sacrifices.

"Speaking of college," Eli said, "I guess we'll all be hearing soon."

"What's everybody's top choice?" Connor asked.

And while they listed their schools—Kansas, Kansas, Vanderbilt, UNC, and Kansas—my mind filled with swaying palm trees, azure waters, golden beaches. Connor had been right to say I'd been craving a fresh start. Could I really turn down the one Mom wanted to hand to me?

9

On my way out of the cafeteria, Lisa caught up with me. "Can I talk to you?"

The last time Lisa sought me out for a conversation, she dropped the bomb that Eli and Jodi had gotten back together. Her words made me nervous.

Lisa must've noticed this, because she laughed. "It's nothing bad. I just wanted to thank you."

"Thank me?" I searched my brain for anything I might have done. "For what?"

"Do you remember back in October when you found Alexis and me fighting about John?"

My face heated at the memory. "Uh, yeah." It had happened the morning after I discovered Eli had fooled around with Jodi at homecoming. I'd completely lost control with my friends, calling them—if memory served correctly—the most self-absorbed people I'd ever met. What a shining moment. Like the total opposite of what Jesus would've done.

"Well, I was kinda mad at you at first, but later I thought about what you said. You know, how it was stupid for Alexis and me to be fighting because I wasn't really in love with John?" Lisa shrugged and popped her gum. "That made a lot of sense to me. And I've been watching you. You really are different now."

I shifted, oddly uncomfortable. "Thanks."

"I mean, the old you never would have put up with Jodi and Eli getting back together." Lisa waved at some guy as he passed by and said to him, "You better let me cheat today. I can't afford another failed test."

"Then maybe you should study," he said with a wink.

Lisa laughed, then turned back to me. "Sorry, what were we talking about?"

I smiled. I'd missed Lisa. Sure, she was ditzy, and her clothes often looked like they'd been spray-painted on, but she had a warmth about her. I always felt accepted around Lisa.

"You were saying the old me would've been mad about Eli and Jodi. I really don't like him anymore, so it's easy."

"But remember before you guys started dating? You were constantly chasing girls away from him, even though you didn't want to date him yourself." Lisa smiled, looking nostalgic. "I used to be like that too with John. But I don't want to do that anymore." She took a deep, cleansing breath, like in yoga. "It's very freeing, you know. Releasing him. Moving on. I stopped feeling sad about school ending. I'm ready for something new. Aren't you?"

Once again the palm trees in my mind swayed in the tropical breeze.

I'd been thirteen my last time in Hawaii. Grammy and Papa lived in a tiny bungalow in Kapaa, Kauai. I remembered that stepping into that house was like stepping back in time—paneled walls and fringed lamp shades. The whole place smelled like dust and mildew, and I couldn't help wrinkling my nose when I walked in. Dad had taken me aside and given me a five-minute lecture about respect.

But the house hadn't mattered much because the only time we spent inside was to sleep. Otherwise Abbie and I were in our bathing suits on the beach. What I wouldn't give to be there now, away from the frozen, barren land of Kansas, away from the drama. It wasn't like going to Hawaii meant staying there forever. Maybe I could just go for the summer, get away for a bit.

But Connor . . .

"I'd be ready for something new, except . . ."

Lisa grinned. "Except for a certain baseball player?"

My face warmed. "Something like that."

"How funny. You spent all of high school hanging out with guys you didn't care about, and now—last semester—you've got Connor." She pointed down a hallway. "Gotta get going. Just wanted to tell you thanks."

"See ya," I said.

As I walked the short distance to study hall, I turned Lisa's words over in my mind. She was right—I had Connor. How could I seriously consider leaving the one person who supported me when most everyone else mocked?

The answer was simple—I couldn't.

❀

"You're quiet," I observed as I drove Abbie and myself home.

Abbie fiddled with a button on her jacket. "That's because I'm trying to figure out how to tell you I'm giving the baby up for adoption."

I stiffened. So she'd decided. Those images I'd indulged—holding my niece for the first time, taking her shopping—wouldn't happen. It had been stupid anyway, letting myself get attached. Hadn't I learned my lesson about not getting my hopes up? But something about babies made it impossible to avoid feeling excited.

"Please don't be mad," Abbie said, and I realized I'd just been sitting there in silence.

"I'm not mad," I assured her. "I'm . . . I don't know what I am."

Abbie's cheeks puffed, then she exhaled long and slow. "Yeah, me neither."

"You wanna talk about it?"

Abbie fingered her seat belt. "It's the same stuff we've said all along. I'm a sophomore in high school, I don't want to be with Lance, and the last thing our house needs is a baby. This way I have the baby March 10 and am back at school by the time spring break is over." She wiped away a tear. "And life goes back to normal."

It sounded so simple when Abbie stated it like that. Sure, just squirt the kid out and head back to school. Like we could ever forget that somewhere in the world, a little piece of my sister would be running around, and yet she would be a complete stranger to us all. The thought chilled me, and maybe it did Abbie too, because she shivered.

"I have an appointment tomorrow with a counselor at Christian Family Services. They said I should bring an adult. Would you mind coming?"

I didn't know if I was exactly what they had in mind when they said an adult, but I said, "Whatever you need."

After the heavy conversation in the car, I hoped Dad had gone to the office so I wouldn't have to face him. We hadn't talked since the day before, and I didn't know how to act around him. He'd cheated on Mom with her best friend and kept it to himself all these years, but it was hard to be too angry with him when at least he was home. These days, Mom seemed eager to cut and run while the rest of us loafed around the house, waiting for her to decide to come home. I no longer knew who deserved my allegiance—the parent who'd screwed up back then, or the one who did now.

I opened the garage door to find Dad standing in the hallway wearing a tight smile. "Hi, girls, how was your day?"

"Fine," we said.

The three of us stood there in the tiny space, just watching each other. Dad's smile grew more strained. "Well. Do you have lots of homework?"

Abbie shrugged. I said, "Some."

He nodded. "I'm ordering takeout, Abbie. You in the mood for anything special?"

"Whatever."

"Or I could attempt to cook."

Abbie didn't smile back. "I'm gonna go lay down."

"Okay, honey." Dad ruffled her auburn hair as she passed, then looked at me. "You have a second to talk?"

I nodded, my mouth dry, and followed him through the kitchen into his office. He pulled the French doors closed behind us.

"I can't get ahold of your mother," he said, turning to face me.

I crossed my arms and leaned against the door frame. "This is news?"

"I wanted to give her the weekend to cool off." Dad ran his hands through his hair. "I didn't even try calling her until today."

"Maybe she needs a little more time. Maybe it'll take her more than a weekend to get over what you did."

When he didn't reprimand me for my lack of respect, I knew he was *really* worried. "Her cell phone isn't working. The recording says it's been disconnected."

"She called me from it yesterday."

Had she possibly already left for Hawaii? She wouldn't do that, right? She wanted Abbie and me with her. At the very least, she'd have said good-bye.

Dad perched on the edge of his desk and said in a matter-of-fact way, "I need to know what she said to you over coffee."

I squirmed. I wanted out of there. "Why?"

"Because I'm trying to put a family back together"—his voice rose with each word—"and I need to know how to reach your mother."

I looked away from him, at a grade-school picture of Abbie's. She had braided pigtails and missing teeth. Why hadn't Dad updated his pictures? Did he prefer to think of us at that age, as little girls who argued with him only when he insisted we go to bed?

"She said I was an accident," I whispered. Mom had said a lot of things. Why choose to tell him that one?

Dad's face paled. "Oh, Skylar, honey. You came along earlier than we planned, but I promise, the moment you were born, neither of us saw you as an accident. When I saw you that first time—"

"It's okay." I was so not in the mood to hear him say anything that might make me like him again. "I don't care. Honestly."

Dad's mouth pressed into a firm line. "Did she say anything else?"

I shook my head. "Can I go start on my homework?"

He nodded.

I'd nearly closed the door, nearly escaped, when Dad called, "Skylar?"

I hesitated—could he tell I'd held back information?

"Would you . . ." He fiddled with his tie. Even on days he worked from home, he usually wore ties. "When she calls you again, would you please say whatever you can to get her back home?"

I nodded. "Sure."

How exhausting, to know before my father that he'd be getting divorced. It's supposed to be a surprise to the kids. Alexis once described her parents' divorce as the shock of a lifetime. My parents, however, seemed eager to consult me with every step.

Jogging up the stairs, I murmured, "Please, God, forgive me for lying." I had no intentions of sweet-talking Mom back home. Why bother? She'd settle in, make fancy dinners for a couple weeks, and then leave again at the next bump in the road. I couldn't keep suffering the pain of losing her. Well, *I* could, but Abbie was a different story. She needed Mom.

Abbie poked her head into my room, wearing a sleeveless shirt despite the frigid January temperatures. "Everything okay?"

She must've heard Dad ask to speak to me in private. "Yeah." I forced a smile. "I think Dad just wanted to make sure you're okay."

She rolled her eyes. "I'm gonna take a nap."

"Okay, sleep well."

When she left, I collapsed onto my bed. I closed my

eyes and tried to remember what life had been like in the little house, when we all shared one and a half baths and two teeny bedrooms. How painful to know those days weren't what I'd thought. If I were Mom, could I forgive Dad for what he'd done? It was hard enough just being his daughter.

My phone rang. Connor.

"Hello?"

"You sound tired."

"Because I'm lying down." I propped myself up. "Better?"

"Much. You miss me on the drive home?"

I chuckled. "It's a miracle I survived the two-minute drive."

"I'm sensing sarcasm," Connor said. "So Jodi tells me you're coming tomorrow night."

"To what?"

"Youth group."

"Oh, right." I glanced at the closed bathroom door. "I can't go."

Connor sighed. "Of course not."

"Do I really deserve that?" I asked. So, yeah, in the past I'd flaked on youth group, but this time I had a reason. A good one.

"It depends on why you can't come."

"I just can't."

Maybe Abbie wouldn't mind me telling Connor about her adoption plans, but I didn't want to take the chance. Only a couple months ago, she'd flown into a violent rage when she discovered I'd told Connor about her pregnancy. Though, for the record, I hadn't *intended* to tell Connor about the baby. He'd overheard me asking Heather to pray for our family. But it had been a moot point to Abbie, who didn't care how word had gotten out, just that it had. Now, for the first time, Abbie and I were getting along. I didn't want to risk spoiling the peace, even if it meant making Connor mad.

"I want a real reason."

"Well, I can't give you one," I said in a cross voice. "You're just going to have to trust me that I can't go."

"You know, it'd be really good for Jodi to see you there. Eli won't come with her."

"Maybe he will. He invited her to church."

"I guess *he* didn't, his mom did. Apparently, she liked how he got involved in church again when he started dating you. She thought if Jodi came, he might."

"Jodi told you this?"

"Eli did. After you left on Sunday."

"Ah."

"So, will you?"

"Will I what?"

"Will you come?"

"I told you—I can't."

"Fine," Connor huffed. "Well, you're not gonna like this, but I told Jodi I'd pick her up."

My heart hammered. "Why? She's got a car."

"I think she's kinda nervous about showing up by herself. I didn't think you'd care because I assumed I'd be taking you as well."

"If I could go, I would. I can't." I took a deep breath. "Will you please do me a favor?"

"You want me to back out of picking her up, don't you?"

Of course I did, but now that he'd guessed it, I felt stupid saying so. I forced myself to take a deep breath. I needed to get my jealousy under control. It had been running rampant since Connor and I had gotten together. I couldn't live like this any longer. Time for rational thinking.

So, worst-case scenario—Jodi truly was after Connor. That didn't mean he was forced to like her back. That all his feelings for me vanished just because she batted her long lashes. I should be totally fine with him taking her to youth group. And I would be.

"Just be careful with her," I said. "She's most lethal when she's being nice."

10

Abbie spoke so quietly, I had to ask her to repeat herself.

"I said, can you just wait out here?" She glanced at me, appearing nervous.

"You don't want me in there?"

She shook her head.

"But . . ." Why didn't she want me in there? "Don't you think you'll want another pair of ears? I mean, they're going to be throwing a lot of information at you."

Abbie shook her head again, her gaze already down the hallway where we expected Cindy Sheldon, the pregnancy counselor, to appear at any moment.

"Well . . . okay." I pulled out *Wuthering Heights*, as if I'd be able to focus.

"Abbie Hoyt?"

A tall woman had appeared in the hall. Her gaze bounced between Abbie and me, the only two people in the waiting room.

"I'm Abbie," my sister said without budging.

If Abbie's age surprised her, the woman did a good job hiding it. But of course Abbie had probably already shared her situation.

The woman stuck out her hand, her clear eyes crinkling with a smile. With her crop of dark hair and fair skin, she looked like a modern-day Snow White. "Hi, Abbie, I'm Cindy." She nodded at me. "Is this a friend of yours?"

A reaction we'd grown used to. Abbie and I shared two things—our last name and a bathroom. She favored our father, fair and auburn, while I carried on Mom's Hawaiian heritage.

"This is my sister, Skylar."

Cindy offered her hand to me as well. "A pleasure to meet you." She turned her smile back to Abbie. "Well, if you girls would follow me, we'll get started."

"Skylar's going to wait out here," Abbie said, her tone leaving no room for disagreement.

A flicker of surprise crossed Cindy's face, but she nodded. "Just make yourself comfortable."

I took this to mean their meeting would take awhile. I settled into my seat in the spacious waiting room, opened *Wuthering Heights*, and hoped to get too absorbed in the world of Catherine and Heathcliff to think about what was happening down that hall.

Sadly, no luck.

The first time I glanced at my cell phone, positive at least thirty minutes had lapsed, only five had. I groaned and considered putting away my book. I'd barely read a page, though I'd been looking at it since Cindy and Abbie disappeared.

The next time I checked, only two more minutes had passed.

I gave up on being a model English student and closed my book. Instead, I preoccupied myself by scrolling through my overgrown contact list. Had I ever cleaned this thing out? Some people I hadn't talked to in over a year.

When I reached the Rs, I saw his name—Aaron Robinson.

My heart raced with the memory.

He'd pulled my cell from my pocket. "Here," he'd said, punching in his number. "For when you get bored with those high school boys." Handing it back to me, he had winked one of his dark eyes.

I'd always been a sucker for dark eyes.

My finger hesitated on the erase button. I longed to call him, to chew him out for the pain he'd caused me. Or nearly caused me. Whatever.

Connor once asked if I'd ever considered that my life might be worse if Aaron hadn't acted like such a scumbag. Would I have ever cleaned up my act and recognized God if not for the wake-up call of Jodi's party?

Really, I should call and thank him.

I smirked at the idea, imagining how it would stun Aaron. Was that why God told us to turn the other cheek? To give our cloak as well as our tunic? Or, to a modern girl like me, my cashmere coat as well as the gorgeous new Armani sweater I'd just bought?

I blinked at my cell phone's screen: DIALING AARON ROBINSON, it informed me. I'd done it. I'd hit the call button.

"Hello?" His voice—quiet and distant because I held the phone in my lap—sent a shiver through me. I'd recognize it anywhere.

"Hello?" he said again. "Who is this?"

I could almost feel his mouth close to my ear, his unshaven chin tickling my cheek. "Let's get out of here," he'd whispered, and I'd wanted to say no, but my mouth felt sticky, like I'd just eaten a spoonful of peanut butter.

"Skylar?" Cindy said, jolting me into the present.

What a relief to find myself not at a raging house party but in the sparsely decorated waiting room of Christian Family Services. I glanced at my cell phone and found the call disconnected. Probably by Aaron, because my finger lingered on the connect button.

Realizing Cindy still watched me, I forced out words. "Sorry, I was just . . ." Just what? "Just . . . thinking."

She gave me a kind smile. "From what your sister's told me, there's a lot to think about these days. Abbie's decided she'd like you to join us." She gestured to my phone. "Would you mind putting it on vibrate? I'd hate for it to disturb us."

"I'll turn it off," I said, fumbling with it as I stood to follow Cindy.

We walked through several short, neutrally painted hallways until finally reaching her office. Though a warm space, it lacked any sort of personal touch. No pictures of her family, no framed finger paintings. Maybe she stashed them under her desk when girls like my sister came in.

Cindy gestured to a corner of the room. Abbie sat on a sofa, her legs crossed at the ankles, which she'd never done until the last couple weeks. She'd gotten too big to comfortably cross at the knees.

Cindy settled into an armchair, and I took a place beside Abbie. A silver bowl of Jolly Ranchers sat on the coffee table. Abbie offered it to me without matching my eye line.

"Abbie tells me you're a senior," Cindy said, pulling a notebook onto her lap.

I unwrapped a green apple candy. "Yeah."

"Do you have plans for college?"

"I'm going to Johnson County."

"I wish they'd make it a four-year college. My daughter went there and loved it. Do you know yet what you want to study?" She glanced at my lace-up boots and patterned skirt. "Maybe design and textiles?"

I smiled politely. "I'm not sure yet."

"Plenty of time to decide. You're very smart to go to community college while you figure it out."

I didn't answer, just kept my smile pasted on. Was I smart or just too lazy to put in the effort of applying to more schools? I didn't know anymore.

Without a graceful segue, Cindy jumped into the reason for the meeting. "Well, Skylar, let me catch you up on what Abbie and I have been discussing. I've explained to Abbie how serious a decision this is. She already knows this, of course, but it's important, especially with how soon her due date is, to move forward from this meeting feeling good about either the decision to put the baby up for adoption or the decision to parent."

Cindy went on to explain how the adoption would work, that Abbie would look through files of families and pick one, but nothing would be final until after the birth of the baby.

I wanted to look at Abbie during this but didn't dare. In my peripheral, it seemed as though her gaze stayed locked on Cindy.

"Any questions so far?" Cindy's gaze flickered between us.

I shook my head.

"Do you get many fifteen-year-olds in here?" Abbie asked, her voice a solid rock.

Cindy offered a kind, closed-mouth smile. "We get women of all ages."

Abbie nodded, apparently satisfied. "And these families who adopt . . . how do you find them?"

"They come to us, actually. They apply, and we do a very thorough evaluation to be sure we can confidently place a child with them."

"Are they mostly people who can't have kids?"

"It varies. Some can't. Some have kids but can't naturally have any more. Others feel called to adopt."

"Called." Abbie shifted in her seat and reached for another Jolly Rancher. "Do the other girls—the mothers—do they usually feel called to give away their baby?"

Cindy shrugged. "Some do. Others simply feel it's the best option." She looked at my sister with such kindness, I wanted to hug her. "It's never an easy decision, though."

Abbie didn't acknowledge this, just popped the candy in her mouth.

"Any other questions?"

Abbie shook her head. "Not right now."

"Then I have a few." Cindy positioned her notepad on the arm of her chair. "You said your parents know about the baby. Is there a reason they aren't here?"

"I . . ." Abbie glanced at me. "I've only told Skylar. About adoption."

"Why's that?"

"Because Mom and Dad want me to keep the baby. They think . . ." Abbie shook her head. "I think they're embarrassed by the idea of adoption. Like doing it is me saying I'd rather have some strange family raise her than either of them."

Cindy cocked her head. "How *do* you feel about your parents being involved in raising the baby?"

Abbie flattened the candy wrapper on her palm, smoothing out the wrinkles as best she could. "They're right, I guess. I'd rather take my chances with a strange family than them."

"That's why?" I said. "Because of Mom and Dad?"

Abbie spared me a glance but quickly returned her attention to Cindy. "Our family's a mess. Seriously. We'd be the worst thing for this baby."

That would've offended me, but I could see Abbie's face—red and tight from restraining tears. And her voice, so defensive. *Too* defensive. Like maybe . . .

"You want to keep her."

Abbie turned to me. Her chin quivered, and a deep crease ran down the bridge of her nose. Just like me when I held back tears.

"It's crazy, I know." Abbie gulped. "I'm fifteen. I've never had a job. I don't have a car. How can I raise a baby?"

Cindy didn't speak. She probably expected me, the big sister, to swoop in with reassurance. She didn't realize how worthless I was whenever words really mattered.

"Do you believe . . ." Abbie toyed with her Jolly Rancher wrapper. "Recently I've felt like God was calling me to raise the baby," she whispered. She looked up at me, her eyes wide and red-rimmed. "Is that possible? After I ignored him and got pregnant? Could he really trust me to raise her, or am I just imagining it because selfishly I want to keep her?"

I glanced at Cindy. I finally had stuff to say, but I couldn't in front of a woman resembling a Disney princess.

Cindy smiled as she stood. "I have something to speak with the receptionist about. Just come find me whenever you're ready."

We watched her leave.

Abbie laughed nervously and balled up the candy wrapper. "She must think I'm a total whack job."

I smiled. "If you're gonna do this, you should probably figure out how to get past what other people think."

"I want to know what *you* think," Abbie said, her eyes searching my face. "Do you think it's possible God is calling me, or am I just being stupid and emotional?"

I turned the Jolly Rancher over in my mouth as I worked to form my thoughts. "Remember over the summer, when I suddenly changed?"

She nodded.

"I'd been at Jodi's party. This guy put something in my drink. He nearly raped me, but Eli followed us and stopped him." I took a deep breath to slow myself down—I'd talked so fast, it'd be a miracle if Abbie had caught half of it. "At first I was naive enough to believe Eli saved me, but I know now God was after me, after my heart."

I placed my hand on Abbie's. "If God is willing to use a kegger of Jodi's to save me, it doesn't seem too crazy to think he might be using her"—I patted Abbie's belly—"to come after you."

Connor called that night as I pulled the blankets around me.

"You just getting home?" I asked, glancing at the clock. 10:30.

"We all went out for pancakes afterward."

I didn't want to ask but couldn't help it. "You all . . . ?"

"Everyone but Cevin. Denny's is funny about dogs."

I breathed a sigh of relief. So much for ceasing to be a paranoid, jealous girlfriend. I mean, so what if Connor *had* gone for pancakes with Jodi? I needed to calm down.

"Why'd you go out for pancakes?" I asked.

"We do this every once in a while. I don't know why. Mom likes 'em a lot, I guess."

I fingered the stitching on my quilt. Abbie had said she didn't mind if I told Connor about the baby, but I didn't know how to broach it. "So, I have something to tell you, but you shouldn't say anything to Chris yet." Connor didn't answer. "Are you there?"

"I'm waiting."

"Abbie and I met with an adoption agency earlier. That's why I wasn't there tonight. She considered giving it up—giving *her* up—but decided not to."

Silence.

"Are you there?"

"Sorry. That time I was thinking. What does this mean for Lance?"

"I don't know. Abbie didn't say, but of course he said he wants to be involved. I'm doubtful." I rolled onto my back and gazed up at the dark ceiling. "At this point, I'm wondering if Hawaii maybe wouldn't be such a bad idea."

"Why do you say that?" Connor asked, his voice guarded.

"A fresh start might be good for Abbie, that's all." I could hear him breathing, but he didn't respond. "Tell me what you're thinking."

"That I don't want to lose you."

"We're not talking about *me* going. We're talking about Abbie," I said.

But my mind filled with palm trees, with golden beaches. With Jodi watching Connor the same way she used to watch Eli.

11

"We missed you on Tuesday," Heather said as we ripped stitches out of old skirts.

"Yeah, Abbie had . . ." *Think, think!* "A baby thing."

Heather didn't seem to notice me bobbling words. "I met your friend Jodi. She's a lot of fun."

I bristled at this. Even Heather? "Yeah."

Heather paused her work and studied my face. "Do you not like Jodi? I thought Connor introduced her as a friend of yours."

So Connor had handled the introductions? I mean, it made sense. He drove her there, she didn't really know anyone else, of course they'd spent time together. I guess I'd been avoiding the idea of how the night might have gone.

I forced out a wooden chuckle. "Yeah, Jodi and I are friends. I just stuck myself with the seam ripper."

"I hate that." She returned to her skirt and I returned to mine. "You think she'll come back on Tuesday?" Heather asked.

Jodi'd had a good time at youth group. She'd jabbered about it a lot on Wednesday. A better person—a nicer person—would have been happy about this. Regardless of how far I'd come since last summer, I still wasn't nice enough to encourage Jodi's spiritual well-being when it meant her spending more time with my boyfriend.

"She really liked it," I said.

Heather beamed, unleashing even more guilt inside me. "Wonderful. I love having seniors there. It's really important for the underclassmen to see."

Okay, enough of this. "Did you ever go out with that guy? The pharmacist or whoever?"

"Yeah." She shook her head. "Nothin'."

"Bummer." Heather went on lots of first dates, but few seconds. "You don't even want to try a second free dinner?"

Heather's face soured and she shook her head, like Curtis did when Amy tried to make him take a bath. "I'm not into recreational dating. If he's not the right one, I'm not interested." She ripped away her final seam with a flourish. "I'd hate to be tied up with Mr. Wrong and miss Mr. Right."

Reaching for strips of red fabric, I thought of how I'd met Connor the day I started dating Eli. Of how Abbie met Chris the same night she'd announced to me she was pregnant. Maybe Abbie and Chris could be together now if only I'd been a better example.

"There's a new doctor working in the NICU who's pretty cute," Heather said with a shrug. "I'm trying to figure out if he's a Christian."

Heather worked as a nurse for moms who'd just had babies. It seemed to me a very noble profession, the encouragement of new life. If only it interested me.

I gave the red corduroy a cross look—I wished I wanted to do more than fuss with clothes. I'd never been passionate about anything else—other than having a good time.

Now it seemed so frivolous. It didn't fit into this new life I hoped to create for myself.

I let the skirt, the fabric swatches, and my scissors fall into a heap on my lap. "I don't think this looks right."

Heather's face pinched into a frown. "What are you talking about? It looks fine."

"It looks . . . I dunno. It just looks wrong."

"That's because it's not finished. You can't look at it when it's half done and expect it to be perfect."

"I guess."

She studied me as I continued to sulk. "You've seemed really frustrated recently. When you first started coming over, you worked circles around me. Now you flit from project to project."

"Just a lot on my mind, I guess."

"Like what?"

Where to begin? The baby who'd take over my house in about seven and a half weeks? My MIA mother, who may or may not be filing for divorce and moving to Hawaii? My recently haunting dreams about lush tropical gardens and surfing? Or my former best friend making herself comfortable with my church and my boyfriend, the two things she knew could hurt me most?

I could trust Heather with these things; she'd proven it to me. She was the first one I'd told about Abbie's pregnancy, about Mom and Dad's marital problems. She'd faithfully prayed for us while keeping her mouth shut.

"My classes are just really hard this semester," I said with a hopefully convincing smile.

So if I knew I *could* trust her, why *didn't* I?

At home, Connor's SUV hogged the driveway.

"What are you doing here?" I asked when I found him seated on a barstool, talking to my father.

He gave me a cheeky grin. "I came for the warm and welcoming atmosphere."

Amazing. I hadn't cracked a genuine smile all day, but somehow this guy could always pull one out of me. "I'm just surprised, is all." I claimed the barstool beside him. "Hi, Daddy."

Dad smiled at me over the top of his glasses. "How was Heather's?"

"Fine."

"What wacky creation did you come home with today?"

I'd ironed the skirt at Heather's, folded it, and nestled it inside my purse. But I said, "It's not ready yet."

Beneath the counter, hidden from my father's eyes, Connor's hand found my knee. "You ready to go?"

"What?"

He gave me a look. "You seriously forgot?"

And then I remembered yesterday, him pointing out that Sunday would be our three-month anniversary. "Unfortunately, I babysit on Sunday nights for Mom and Dad's Bible study," he'd said, "so could we go out Saturday night instead?"

And somehow I'd forgotten. Eli hadn't exactly wined and dined me. He'd apparently exhausted all chivalry during his three-year, off-and-on pursuit.

"Of course I didn't forget." I squeezed his hand beneath the counter. "Just let me get changed."

"You'll want something warm," Connor called after me.

Something warm? Where was he taking me? Ice fishing?

Dressing both cute and warm seemed impossible. I tried on four different sets of light layers. They all made me look ten pounds heavier than when I'd come upstairs. Of course, I'd be wearing my down coat, which turned me into a powder blue snowman. But why should I care? This was *Connor*. The guy appeared to own a thousand pairs of identical Adidas tear-aways.

I scowled at my puffy reflection and trotted downstairs.

My father had returned to work, and Connor stood in the living room, looking at baby pictures of Abbie and me. He tapped on the picture of my first Easter. "That's a big, frilly dress."

I made a face. "Someone should've called child services on them."

Connor chuckled and turned to me. "Wow, you look beautiful."

"I do?" I looked down at my wool sweater and cords. "I feel puffy."

"No, you're cute." He pinched my side. "Wow. You took me seriously about dressing warm."

"Well, you haven't told me what we'll be doing, so I didn't know how seriously to take you. But Connor, this is supposed to be a date, an important date, and right now I just feel disgusting—"

He clamped his hand over my mouth, his eyes shining. He apparently found my frustration amusing. "No more crazy talk. Even with another ten layers, you'd still be head and shoulders above any other girl."

My face heated with the compliment. All my life, guys had told me I was beautiful and it never did a thing for me. But with Connor, sometimes he just looked at me and I felt all warm and gooey inside. Like the molten lava cakes Amy Ross made, with the firm outside and runny chocolate centers.

After kissing me, Connor held up a necktie.

I looked from it to him. "I know I wear some outrageous stuff, but that really clashes with my sweater."

Connor rolled his eyes. "It's a blindfold so you don't know where we're going. I'm trying to be romantic. Now turn around so I can tie it."

After triple-checking to make sure I couldn't see, Connor finally led me out to the car. I took several guesses along the way—that park out south he kept saying he wanted to take me to, the lake, the Plaza for a carriage ride.

"Ooh, that would've been a good one. I'll have to save that for another anniversary," Connor said as the road got suddenly bumpy, like we were driving on gravel.

I gripped my seat. "How long since we left my house? Did you take me out to the country?"

"Nope." The car slowed to a stop. "Go ahead and take it off."

I pulled down the blindfold. "Why would you bring me here?"

"Why would I bring you here?" Connor laughed. "This is where we met."

I made a face. "But I was so rude to you."

"Well, I looked for a place in Kansas City where you weren't, but I couldn't find one."

I backhanded him in the chest. "Low blow."

"I'm kidding," he said. "Come on."

He retrieved several blankets and a brown Planet Sub sack from the backseat. We walked across the gravel parking lot to the dusty, vacant fields.

"It's strange like this," Connor said. "I didn't think it'd be this eerie."

I thought about the previous Sunday, when I'd frozen on the bleacher and hung up on Connor for mentioning Jodi.

He glanced at me. "If you want to go somewhere else, we can."

I shook my head. "It's perfect."

Connor spread one of the blankets onto a bleacher before we sat. At the bite of the wind, he said, "At least there won't be any bugs."

I yanked at the zipper of my coat. "That's one way to look at it."

"Creamy club," he said, handing over my foil-wrapped sandwich. He noticed me staring at him. "Isn't that what you get?"

"Yeah, I . . ." It touched me that he knew that kind of stuff, what I ordered at specific restaurants. Would my friends know? Would my family? That Connor cared enough to pay attention made us feel real, like we could be this way—him and me—for a while. For forever. But this seemed like kind of a lot to throw at him.

"I just didn't know you knew," I said.

He smiled. "Of course I know."

I took a bite of my sandwich and observed the frosty field. "This time of year, it's always a little hard for me to remember what summer feels like. Free time, warmth, green. It's always a little hard to believe that it'll all come back."

"Are you really that cold? 'Cause we can eat in the car."

"No, I'm fine." I wiggled my toes inside my shoes, making sure they hadn't fallen off. "But you should probably ask me again in five minutes."

Connor smiled and smoothed my wind-whipped hair from my face. "So, what'd you think of me that first night we met?" He held up a hand to keep me from answering. "Let me guess. You thought, Where have you been all my life?"

I laughed. "How'd you know?"

"I have a hunch about these things."

I took several bites of my sandwich. "This is really good. Thank you."

"You know, I was serious about the question." His gloved fingers caressed my hair again, creating static cling. "About what you thought of me that first night."

He really wanted an answer? But why? Surely he knew my initial thoughts of him hadn't been flattering.

"Well, it was the first night after . . ." I didn't say it. Aaron was someone we never, ever talked about. "You seemed overbearing, but I think I just wasn't in a place to meet anybody new. Especially a guy."

Connor didn't seem offended. "I probably *was* overbearing. I knew I needed to say hi to you, that it'd be weird if Eli came back and I hadn't, but you were so . . ." He tipped his head from side to side as if searching for the right word. With each tip, my stomach wound tighter. I assumed he was searching for a way to avoid insulting me.

"Just say it," I said into my sandwich.

Connor sighed. "It's embarrassing. You'll think I'm shallow."

"No more shallow than me."

He sighed again. "You were intimidatingly beautiful."

There he went, making me all gooey inside. "That's what you thought?"

He nodded, his gaze never straying from my face. "But of course I didn't want you knowing I was intimidated, so I probably seemed freakishly friendly."

I chuckled at the memory of Connor thrusting out his hand for me to shake. He'd yammered on and on about why Eli was giving him a ride home, about how he'd lived in Kansas City once before. In my perfect hindsight, his nerves were obvious.

"Well, don't worry," I said. "I had no idea you felt that way."

Connor pantomimed wiping sweat off his forehead. Then his expression became serious. "Now you've become intimidatingly beautiful in *here* as well." He pressed his gloved fingertips into my sternum.

Even through my puffy jacket, wool sweater, thermal tees, and long underwear, my skin tingled where he'd touched me. I didn't feel so beautiful inside these days, not with that prick of jealousy I'd felt when Eli and Jodi got back together. Or how I really, really didn't want Jodi coming to my church.

My eyes misted as I leaned to kiss him. The buzzing of my phone interrupted our tender moment.

Connor rested his forehead against mine. "This is what I get for dating a popular girl, I guess."

"I'll just push them into voice mail," I said, but that's

before I saw a Kansas City number I didn't recognize. Mom?

I opened my phone. "Hello?"

"Hi, sweetie."

I looked at Connor. "Hi, Mom," I said for his benefit. His eyes rounded, and he gave my leg a pat before returning to his sandwich.

"I'm sorry I haven't been in contact with you this week. I've been busy."

"With what?" But did I want to know?

"Just . . . stuff. Preparations."

My muscles clenched at this word. "Preparations" made it sound as though divorce and Hawaii were a go.

"You have a new number," I said in an icy voice. What if I'd needed to get ahold of her? What if Abbie went into preterm labor? A mother should always be reachable.

"It was only a matter of time before Paul started calling, and I just can't deal with him yet."

Paul. She didn't even have the courtesy to refer to him as my father anymore. Like I was some girlfriend rather than her daughter.

"Mom, you need to talk to him. You can't just file for divorce and move to Hawaii."

"That's not for you to comment on," Mom said. "I'm not asking your advice. I'm your mother."

I didn't respond. Connor poured me a cup of hot chocolate. I sipped it, wishing I hadn't answered the phone, that Dad had kept his dirty secret, that I didn't understand both sides of this argument.

"Have you given our discussion any more thought?" Mom asked. "About moving to Hawaii, I mean."

Connor apparently heard Mom. He looked at me, his eyes even bigger than usual.

"Mom, you know that's a crazy idea. I'm almost done with senior year, and Abbie's, like, thirty-two weeks pregnant."

Connor nodded and patted my leg again.

Mom sighed. "I guess it doesn't make much sense. It was wishful thinking on my part." She clucked her tongue several times, the way she often did when brainstorming. "What about when school's out? College in Hawaii is just the same as college here. I could help Abbie with the baby. It makes perfect sense."

I swallowed, my eyes never leaving Connor's. "My life is here, Mom. I can't just leave."

"Take it from me, Skylar," Mom said, quiet and venomous. "It's not worth it to rearrange your entire life for a guy. *Especially* in high school. Did you know only 4 percent of people marry their high school sweethearts? With those odds, is it worth it to give up what I'm offering?"

Still Connor and I watched each other. I thought of these past months, about how whenever Mom left, Connor was always around to help me sort it out. About the guy who knew I ordered the creamy club at Planet Sub, who brought hot chocolate. And the woman who ordered me plain coffee at Starbucks.

"I'm not coming with you," I said. "Please stop asking."

I wasn't sure who hung up first.

In my dream, I'm wearing a fabulous white-on-black polka-dot swimsuit, a throwback to the twenties. The breeze

*tastes salty. The gorgeous sound of cresting waves fills my
ears.*

"Like this," Abbie says.

*I turn to find my sister—slim and smiling—twisting her
feet deep into the golden sand.*

"Where's the baby?" I ask.

*Abbie cups her ear, the universal sign for not being able
to hear.*

*"Where's the baby?" I yell, even though she's standing
right next to me.*

She screws up her face. "We left it in Kansas."

*Panic floods me. "We can't leave her! We have to go
back!"*

*Abbie shakes her head. "It's not your baby, Skylar. It's not
your responsibility."*

*"We shouldn't be here!" I yell, trying to dig my way out
of the sand.*

*Abbie turns and surveys the ocean, the surfers, the trees.
"Why would you be anywhere else?"*

And then I woke up.

12

"Can I talk to you?"

I looked up from my textbook to find Eli standing beside my table. I glanced around the library at my fellow study hall classmates.

Eli grinned, making his dimples pop. "Don't worry. I told Ms. Ness we're working on an American History project together."

"Right," I said with a smile of my own. "That history project."

He took the seat across from me and glanced at my open textbook. "Were you actually working?"

"Yeah, but it's fine."

"You're the only senior I know who's trying this semester." Eli cocked his head and studied me. "Which seems odd for you."

"I don't know why I'm doing it, honestly." I cast a forlorn look at my boring, boring bio book. "I don't need help getting into Jo Co, it's not going to bring up my overall GPA by much, and there's plenty of other stuff I'd rather be doing."

"You've changed a lot since I met you," Eli said, turning my highlighter over in his hands. "That's kinda what I want to talk to you about."

"Yeah?"

"Yeah." Eli flicked my highlighter so it spun in circles on the table. He always fidgeted when nervous. "Jodi seems to be going through the same thing you did last summer. She's talking about getting out of the party scene and asking lots of big questions. It's weird. First you, now her." He gave me a wry smile. "Must be something I do to girls."

"I don't think it's about you," I said.

Eli shrugged. "Maybe not." He stared off vacantly. "I just don't know what to do."

My heart thudded as I realized he was going to break up with her. I shouldn't feel that stab of victory—I knew they wouldn't last!—but couldn't help it. Here Jodi had wrangled him away from me, and now she was about to lose him for the same reasons.

"So I guess what I'm wondering is"—Eli sucked in a breath—"what could I have done to be better for you? I really want to be there for Jo."

It infuriated me, it really did. Jodi was worth supporting, but I wasn't? So, maybe I hadn't been the best girlfriend. And yeah, maybe I'd spent a lot of time wishing I was with Connor instead. But still. Eli may as well have walked up and slapped me in the face.

"Um." I turned back to my bio book. "I don't know, honestly."

Eli worked at bending a paper clip out of shape. "She wants me to get more involved at church. When she told me that, it was like . . . what's that word? That French word, meaning something repeating itself?"

"Déjà vu?"

"Yeah. Déjà vu. I thought it might be this phase of hers,

111

although I'm not sure why. I thought it was a phase with you, and . . ." Eli gestured to me. "Well, obviously it's not. You haven't taken a drink since that night, and you're even *studying*."

Kinda made me sound lame. Not that I cared.

"Is it really so bad if this isn't just a phase of Jodi's?" I asked. "I mean, am I, like, disgusting to you or something?"

Eli grinned, ever charming. "Of course not. You know I think you're great, Skylar."

Heaven help me, I loved hearing him say that.

"And Jodi's great," he rushed to add. He dropped his gaze to the now useless paper clip. "I just want to be there for her, you know? That's how I lost you, letting Connor be there for you when I should've been. I don't want the same thing to happen with Jodi."

I tapped my pen against the table as I thought. I could feel the slight twitch of my left eye as I mulled over Eli's words. "You ever get worried? About Jodi and Connor, I mean."

Eli frowned. "To be honest, it was a little weird at first. Another case of . . . what's that word again?"

"Déjà vu."

"Right. I worried about Jodi falling for Connor like you did, but then I thought about how good everything worked out."

"What do you mean?"

"Like, it sucked when I found out you and Connor were together, but aren't we happier this way? Me with Jodi and you with Connor?" He shrugged. "I dunno. Maybe it doesn't make any sense, but at this point, I figure if I'm meant to be with Jodi, things will work out."

An attitude I could stand to learn from, considering

that my paranoia about Jodi and Connor made me into the exact kind of girlfriend I didn't want to be.

The bell rang, and I collected my things. "I think Jodi'd just appreciate having you around. Like at church and youth group and stuff."

Eli nodded. "I told her I'd go to that winter retreat thingy."

"The what?"

"Oh. She said Connor was going. I assumed you were as well. I'm pretty sure it's the last weekend of February."

I racked my brain—nothing. "What is it?"

"Remember, we went freshman year? They have it at that retreat center in rural Missouri. We did a lot of hand-holding and singing 'Kumbaya.'" He grinned. "Not really, but it was pretty bad."

"Sounds vaguely familiar."

"I swore I was done with all that stuff, but Jodi really wants to go." Eli shrugged. "I guess that means I'll be there."

I bit my lower lip. "I wonder why Connor didn't tell me about it."

I didn't realize I'd spoken out loud until Eli said, "Maybe he forgot."

"Yeah, maybe." I hitched my bag higher on my shoulder as we exited the library.

"How are things going with you and Connor?"

"Things are . . ." What was an appropriate word to use with your ex-boyfriend? One that didn't sound too braggy but also didn't make him think you regretted losing him? "Nice."

He grinned—dimples, crinkled eyes, the works. I tried not to notice how good he looked.

"That doesn't sound very convincing," Eli said. He threw

an arm around my shoulder, buddy-like. Though the little flip my heart did didn't feel very buddy-like. "Do I need to have a talk with him?"

"No, things are good, I just . . ." I didn't know how to tell Eli his girlfriend was causing problems. "Sometimes I get the feeling that—"

The sound of Abbie's voice—Abbie's loud, angry voice— distracted me.

"Just talk to me!" she yelled from somewhere nearby. "Through this whole thing, I haven't asked you a single favor. I'm asking you now—talk to me."

It sounded like it came from around the corner. I sprinted that direction, even though I knew Abbie was more than capable of taking care of herself.

I pushed my way through the crowd surrounding my sister and Lance. Lance just stood there in the circle, his eyes darting about, as if looking for someone to rescue him from the big, scary pregnant girl. Only at school did I notice the size of Abbie's belly. Something about the lockers, the teachers, and the other stick-skinny girls drew attention to it.

"If you don't want to help, that's fine. But have the guts to say it to my face. Don't make me hear it from Marie Green." Abbie pushed him, and the girl next to me giggled. I shot her a look that shut her up, but I didn't blame her for laughing. It really was a sight, Lance getting harassed by my eight-months-pregnant sister.

"Take him out, Abbie!" some girl in the crowd hollered. More giggling.

Okay, as much as I hated to rescue Lance, I had to get Abbie calmed down. The doctor said stress was really bad for the baby.

I cupped Abbie's arm and prodded her away from Lance, whom she'd nearly pinned against the wall. She whirled to face me, anger flashing in her eyes. It cooled at the sight of me. "He thought I'd give her away." Her chin trembled. "*That's* why he's been nice."

She teetered on the edge of a breakdown, I could see it. Abbie had always been emotional, but now those emotions swung like a pendulum—furious one second, devastated the next. On Christmas, she had been laughing at something Connor said when her giggles suddenly became hysterical tears, just like I'd seen happen on TV.

"Let's just go, okay?" I said in a low voice.

"Not until he talks to me." She crossed her arms over her chest, resting them on her swollen stomach. She glared at Lance. "I want to hear you say it, that you're not gonna help."

His Adam's apple bobbed. "Let's talk about this in private."

"No. We're going to talk about it right here. Tell me." She poked him. "Tell me what you told Marie Green."

Lance looked at me like, *Can't you do anything?*

"It'll be over a lot quicker if you just tell her," I said.

He shuffled his feet. "My parents said you can have all the financial help you want—"

Abbie snorted. "Financial help. Great. *That's* what I need." She poked him again. "Do you know how much money my father makes? I'm not hurting for 'financial help,' Lance."

He scowled at her mocking tone. "You know, *you* decided to keep the baby. I told you I thought adoption was a good idea."

"You said to do whatever I thought was best."

"Because I thought you knew it was best to give it up."

"*Her*," Abbie said. "My baby's a girl. And I can raise her just fine, thank you. Without you and without your parents' guilty money."

"You're being stupid, Abbie," Lance said, but he took a couple steps back when someone else entered the circle.

Eli pushed Abbie and me back, getting right in Lance's face. "You talk to her like that again and you'll live to regret it." Eli towered over him until Lance had the good sense to turn away. "In fact, if you talk to her *at all*, you'll regret that too."

Lance muttered, "Whatever," and weaseled out of the circle.

I tucked my arm around Abbie. "C'mon, let's go," I said, leading her off toward the senior parking lot.

Over Abbie's head, my eyes met Eli's. "Thank you," I mouthed, and when he smiled—so sincere, so sweet—I remembered why, not so long ago, he'd been one of my best friends.

In the car, the pendulum swung.

"I just can't believe this," Abbie managed to say through sobs. "I can't do this alone, I can't. Everyone is right. I should give her up for adoption."

"The only person saying that is Lance, and that's just because he's afraid to take responsibility."

She leaned on my shoulder. "He's been avoiding me since I told him I decided to keep her. I knew he didn't really want to help, but still, when I found out all that stuff from Marie . . ." Abbie looked at me through puffy eyes. "They were at a party together, and he was hitting on her. She asked about me, and he said . . ."

More sobbing. I squeezed her as tight as I could in our awkward position. I'd thought I could get her home before the crying started, but I'd barely gotten the keys in the ignition.

Abbie drew back from me and took a deep breath. "He said that he always thought I'd 'do the responsible thing' and get rid of the baby, but since I wasn't going to, there was no need for him to have to pay too. His parents don't want him getting mixed up in it. Worried about it ruining his chances for an athletic scholarship." Abbie swiped away her tears. "Isn't that awful? Chris was willing to help me with the baby, and she isn't even his."

"Lance is an idiot," I said. *"Lance is an idiot"? Really? That's the best I can come up with?* "I'm gonna be here for you," I added.

"You shouldn't have to be." Abbie stroked her belly. "Lance is right. I'm the one who made this decision. I can't expect everyone else to pay for it."

"We're sisters," I said. "We stick together."

A thin smile stretched across her face. She relaxed her head against the seat and surveyed the parking lot. "You ever think how nice it'd be to get out of here?"

I picked at the hem of my sweater. "Sometimes."

She rolled her head to face me. "Where do you think Mom is?"

"I don't know." *God, forgive me.*

"Dad must've done something really bad."

"Maybe." I made sure she couldn't see the tick of my left eye. "Or maybe Mom's blowing it out of proportion."

"She does have a flair for the dramatic."

I arched my eyebrows. "Like someone else I know."

Abbie grinned. "It must've been quite a sight in there, huh?"

"Until Lance leaves for college, he'll be hearing about that time Abbie Hoyt nearly beat him up when she was pregnant."

She giggled. What a refreshing sound. "Yeah, I was about to pop him one. Good timing on Eli's part."

I thought of Jodi's party, of Eli bursting into the guest room as Aaron loomed over me. "He has a knack for that."

Silence settled over the car, then in a voice barely over a whisper, Abbie asked, "He really kept you from being raped?"

I swallowed and nodded. "If it hadn't been for Eli . . ." I shrugged.

Abbie exhaled slowly. "I can't believe . . ." She shook her head. "You must be so grateful to him."

I shifted in my seat. My gratefulness had gotten me in trouble last summer when I decided it was a good enough reason to date Eli. "He's a good friend."

Now Abbie's eyebrows raised. "He seems to be hovering around you lately. You sure that's all he is?"

His words lingered in my mind, about how everything worked out for the best, him being with Jodi, and me with Connor. Clearly he had no intentions of trying to win me back.

I nodded at Abbie. "Definitely."

"You sure you're okay?" Connor asked as I drove us home.

I nodded. "Mm-hmm."

He looked over his shoulder at Abbie. "So I hear I should stay on your good side."

"Yeah, I'm dangerous." I heard the smile in her voice.

"Sounds like it." He glanced at me as we came to a four-way stop. To Abbie he said, "Would you mind protecting me a little later? I think your sister's got it in for me."

"I told you I'm fine," I said.

"Yeah, but you're lying."

I turned left. In about thirty seconds I'd have him out of my car.

"The real trouble is"—Connor tossed his feet onto my dashboard—"I'm mad at you now."

"You're mad at me?" I laughed. "What'd I do?"

"Instead of talking about whatever it is that's bothering you, you're pretending it's all okay."

When I looked at him, I saw that he was very, very serious.

I swallowed. "Maybe I'm just not ready to talk about it yet. Isn't that allowed?"

"Sure. But tell me *that*."

I accelerated into the Rosses' driveway and jabbed the brake, giving everyone a little whiplash.

"Hey, unborn child back here, if you don't mind," Abbie said as she rubbed her belly.

I glared at Connor. "Bye."

He showed no signs of exiting. "Why do you have to make everything so hard?"

"Let's give them privacy," Chris said to Abbie. They unfastened their seat belts and left us there in the car.

119

"Do you always have to bring stuff up in front of them?" I asked. "It makes me uncomfortable."

"I don't mean to make you uncomfortable. I just want to sort this out." Connor reached for my hand. "I hate it when you're mad at me. I'd like to get it over with as soon as possible."

I turned off the ignition and took a deep breath. "Why didn't you tell me about the winter retreat?"

He blinked rapidly. "Are you serious? *That's* what you're mad about?"

I shifted in my seat. "Well . . . Eli said that Jodi said you're going, and I don't understand why you didn't tell me about it." I cringed and buried my head in my hands. "I can't believe I just said that. That's how far I've sunk? To a 'he said, she said' fight?"

Connor's fingers grazed my cheek. "Skylar . . ." I forced myself to peek at him. "What's really going on?"

"I don't know," I murmured.

"Why are you so worried about Jodi and me? It's like you said—I'm not Eli."

"I know you're not—"

"Do you? Because you say you trust me, but you're not really acting like it."

"Look at my life," I said, louder than intended. I lowered my voice to a normal volume. "Look at my friends, what happened with John and Lisa. Then me and Eli. And now this thing with my parents." I fiddled with the tassels of my scarf. "And did you know only 4 percent of people marry their high school sweethearts?"

Connor sighed. "Skylar, your mom said that to manipulate you into doing what she wants. For all we know, she made up that number."

I shook my head. "I looked it up. Four percent get married. Two percent stay that way."

"Okay, I'm confused." Connor raked his hands through his hair. "Are we arguing about me and Jodi or the odds of us working out?"

I didn't know anymore. "It doesn't matter."

"Yeah, it does. I need to know the best way to answer you."

"It doesn't matter," I said again. I reached to turn the ignition. "I'm being stupid. Let's just drop it."

His hand covered mine, preventing me from starting the car. "I don't know how this is going to work out, Skylar. You're my best friend and I love you, but I think we're both smart enough to know a lot could happen between now and when we're ready to get married."

I cringed. "Please don't think I'm trying to get a promise ring out of you or something—"

"I'm not done." He gave me a searing look. "I need to make sure you know I'm never, ever going to cheat on you. Even if I was given the opportunity. Even if I knew for sure you'd never find out about it. Tell me you know that."

"I know that. But—"

"Are you just saying you know that, or do you really know that?"

I sighed. "I'm not sure."

He fit his arm around my shoulders, a smile tugging at the corners of his mouth. "Well, at least you're being honest."

"I'm acting crazy and I know it." I leaned against him, ignoring how the emergency brake wedged into my ribs. "I've never felt this way about anybody. I guess it's messing with my head."

"I honestly forgot to mention the winter retreat. Since you go to church there—"

I covered his mouth with my hand. "You have nothing to apologize for."

The car grew cold as we lingered. I opened my mouth to suggest moving inside—the brake was really uncomfortable—when Connor said, "I've got a confession that might make you feel better."

I pulled back so I could see his face. "Yeah?"

"I felt a little jealous when I heard Eli came to Abbie's rescue." His ears pinked. "I wished I'd been there to help."

"It's more like he came to Lance's rescue."

He grinned back at me, then his smile faltered. "Well, all the same. Eli's been hanging around you a lot recently, and you guys have a history."

Hmm. In the last couple hours, two people had commented on Eli hanging around. Had he been? We'd eaten lunch together for the last week—he'd sat by me twice—but of course everyone had been there. Including Connor and Jodi. And maybe once or twice we'd been headed the same direction and walked together, but all that didn't amount to anything, did it?

Even if it did, I wasn't interested.

I ruffled Connor's coarse hair. "You don't need to be worried."

"Neither do you," he said, and it surprised me how much I trusted him.

13

"See, it's not as bad as you remembered, is it?" Connor asked, poking me.

I helped myself to a couple fluffy sugar cookies. "Please stay at least three feet from me at all times. You smell like you just ran ten miles."

Connor took an exaggerated whiff of me. "You smell purdy."

"Ew. I think you just dripped sweat on me." I wiped at my shoulder. "I'm serious. Three feet."

I turned from the snack table to find a seat. Across the church auditorium, Jodi waved wildly, beckoning to the table where she and Eli already sat. Super.

"Go on," Connor said, filling two cups with Dr Pepper. "I'm right behind you."

What option did I have? We were the only seniors who'd shown at youth group. It would look a little weird if I plopped down with Chris and his friends. Maybe I could get away with it if Abbie had come, but she'd dropped out of youth group stuff back when she started showing.

"So. Are you too cool to play Ultimate Frisbee with us?" Eli asked. He also shimmered with sweat.

I popped a bite of cookie into my mouth. "Pretty much."

Too unathletic was more like it. Simple Frisbee tossing was too much for me. That made running, catching, and that weird two-step rule out of the question. I didn't need to humiliate myself in front of a room full of underclassmen, thank you very much.

"You should've played, Skylar," Jodi said. Oddly, she looked shower fresh. "It was fun."

"It's a losing battle, guys," Connor said as he joined us. He left a seat between us, respecting my three-foot rule. When I'd insisted on that, I hadn't expected Eli's and Jodi's surprised expressions.

"You can sit next to me," I said.

"No, no, no." Connor held up his hands, palms out. "You said three feet."

Jodi giggled. "Why?"

"Apparently I smell."

"*I* don't think you smell."

Oh, come on!

Connor glanced at me. "I probably smell a little." The way he smiled at me, reassuring and loving, made my heart soar.

A pair of pinking shears clattered in front of me, and I looked up to see Heather grinning. "Probably kinda hard to work without those, huh?"

I hadn't even noticed they'd been missing. "Yeah, thanks."

"Heather, I love your necklace," Jodi said, her voice sugary.

Heather beamed as she fingered the beads. "Thanks."

"Did you make it yourself?"

"I made the strand, but my dad bought the pendant on a business trip in India."

"I'd love to know how to make my own jewelry."

I could see it coming but had no way to stop it.

"Why don't you come over on Saturday?" Heather asked, her voice pure sunshine. "Skylar and I get together to sew. We could do jewelry too."

"That sounds great." Jodi gave me a cautious smile. "Unless Skylar minds."

So she wasn't content just to take Connor from me. She wanted everything I'd come to value. And my mind worked too blasted slow to think of a way to derail her.

I matched her phony smile for phony smile. "Why would I mind?"

I hurried toward my locker on a mission to retrieve *Wuthering Heights*. I'd totally spaced bringing it to study hall and needed every free second if I wanted to ace my test the next day.

When I rounded the hallway, I found Jodi already standing at her locker. Great.

"Hey."

"Hi."

Neither of us smiled. No need to pretend.

"I forgot a book," I said. Like I needed to explain myself to her.

"I'm ditching."

"Ah." I spun in my combination. The silence made me uneasy. "So. You think you'll keep coming to youth group?"

I felt her watching me. "Why?"

"Just curious." I focused on my row of textbooks. "I think it's good. That you're coming, I mean."

125

"Huh." She filled in her lips with a peach-colored gloss. "I kinda got the feeling you didn't want me there."

"That's not true," I lied.

"Don't worry about it. I get it." Jodi pressed her lips together, then wiped away the gloss that dared to stray outside her lip line.

"You get what?"

"Why you're nervous. You think I'm after Connor."

"No I don't."

Why couldn't I confront her? Just say that I didn't *think* she was after Connor, I *knew* she was?

Jodi leaned against her locker and smirked. "How'd it feel when Eli and I got back together?"

I rolled my eyes. "I don't care about you and Eli."

"I think you do. Or did, anyway." She crossed her arms. "I think you felt jealous. Why else would you have purposefully ignored him the first day back at school?"

I looked away. If only I'd said hi to Eli that day. If I'd foreseen the triumphant sheen in Jodi's eyes, I'd have tried harder. "It just surprised me, is all. But I wasn't jealous."

"Sure." She examined me. "Just like I'm sure you won't feel a little twinge of happiness when I tell you I'm breaking up with him."

I *did* feel a twinge of happiness, of victory. How dare she know those ugly parts of me so well. "But I just talked to Eli on Monday. It sounded like everything is going really well."

"I guess it is. He's a nice enough guy and all, but I'm just . . ." She shrugged. "Well, I'm into someone else."

My left eye twitched like crazy. She didn't possibly mean . . .

Jodi's mouth quirked in a half smile. "Sound familiar?"

"He's not interested in you," I said through gritted teeth. "He told me so."

"Funny." She floated past me, on her way back to wherever she came from. "When I was dating Connor, he told me the same thing about you."

Jodi's words pounded in my brain as I rushed to Connor's English class. Why had she told me she liked him? Surely she knew the first thing I'd do was tell him, and then both of us would be on our guards against her flirtatious ploys.

Unless she *knew* I'd tell him and it was all part of her plan . . .

My ballet flats skidded against the linoleum as I stopped. Should I *not* tell Connor? Would telling him somehow force him closer to Jodi in a way I couldn't predict?

I paced the width of the hall several times. It seemed to me that telling Connor could only help our situation. At least he'd know I wasn't being paranoid, that Jodi really was after him. And if I didn't tell him now, it would likely come out later in some heated argument.

Maybe *that's* what Jodi had anticipated—me losing my cool and blowing up about it. Well, I'd show her. I'd explain everything to Connor in a perfectly calm, rational way.

I hunted down his English class, fibbed him out of there, and waited for him to join me in the hall.

"What's going on?" he asked, forehead creased with concern.

"C'mon." I dragged him around the corner so his teacher wouldn't notice our loitering.

"I have a test tomorrow," Connor said, "so if this isn't important, I need to get back in there."

"Why would I pull you out of class if it wasn't important?" I asked, then unloaded my entire conversation with Jodi.

He frowned all the way through it.

"*Now* do you believe me that she's after you?" I asked.

"It just doesn't make sense." He tugged at the drawstrings of his hoodie. "At youth group last night she said—"

"Don't you see that everything she's saying is just to get to you? You can't trust her." So much for sounding calm and rational.

Connor sighed. "As I was saying, last night she told me she's thinking about breaking up with Eli, but because she thinks he's wrong for her."

"She must've told you that just to gauge your reaction." I thought of Jodi studying me, searching for signs of happiness.

He considered this. "Or maybe when she said she's into someone else, she didn't mean me."

I rolled my eyes. "Who then? Jesus?"

He shrugged. "Maybe."

"No, because she said you'd told her you weren't interested in me."

"When did I say that? Of course I'm interested in you."

"Not now. When you and Jodi were dating."

"Oh." A crease formed on the bridge of his nose as he thought. "Right, I'd forgotten about that. She was jealous that Cameron and Curtis liked you better than her. Who, by the way, miss you and want you to come by the house."

So not the time. I tapped my foot, impatient. "What are we gonna do about this?"

"About Jodi?" He shrugged. "What's there to do? The absolute worst-case scenario is she likes me. That doesn't change how I feel about you."

Relief flooded me. When he put it like that, it sounded so sensible. This wasn't junior high. Jodi's liking him didn't have to affect his feelings.

I sagged against the wall, against the large painting of our school creed. "I guess you're right."

"I'm always right," he teased, taking my hand and squeezing it.

I fixed him with a serious look. "Please promise me you'll be careful."

He pressed a kiss onto my hand as a smile crept onto his face. "Sorry, girl. You can't get rid of me so easy."

14

Observing our lunch table dynamics, I wondered why people seemed to want whatever they couldn't have. Even when they'd had and rejected it, oh, a million times before.

Case in point: John practically salivated as he leaned toward Lisa. "So I went to P.F. Chang's last night, Lisa. Remember that time I ordered the Kung Pao and you didn't know how hot those peppers were?"

Lisa smiled politely. "Mm-hmm."

"I hadn't been there since then."

"Yeah, me neither." Lisa turned to Connor. "Hey, you lived in Vegas, right?"

As the two fell into a discussion about best and worst casino buffets, I watched John fidget with the remains of his pizza. He couldn't keep his eyes off Lisa. Even before he and Alexis broke up last week, there'd been indications that he liked Lisa again. Now he appeared incapable of hiding it, even with Alexis sitting at the table.

Alexis seemed to be doing her best not to pay attention to John. She turned her back to him and spoke to Jodi, who appeared grateful for an excuse to ignore Eli's sulking. He'd been acting like this all week, ever since she broke up with him. Yeah, we'd clearly crossed the line into incestuous. Time to move on to college, to find new friends.

"How's the pizza?" I asked Eli, who sat beside me. Not the cleverest of conversation starters, but I wanted to say something.

"Fine."

"Doesn't look like it's swimming in grease, you know?"

"Yep."

Okay, fine. We didn't need to talk. I'd just been trying to do him a favor.

I returned my attention to eating rather than distracting him. My gaze involuntarily flickered Jodi's direction. She smirked and turned back to Alexis. In Jodi's twisted world of revenge, she probably interpreted my talking to Eli as flirting in hopes of making her jealous. And Eli being tight-lipped looked like a rebuff.

Oh, if I wanted to make her jealous, I could. In five minutes I could have him wrapped back around my finger, vanquishing any desire he had for Jodi.

I grinned at Eli, warm and inviting. I opened my mouth to speak, but nothing came out.

He raised his eyebrows. "What?"

I swallowed my baiting words and turned back to my sandwich. "Never mind," I whispered.

"You sure?"

I nodded, careful to keep my gaze averted. Tears burned my eyes, and I didn't want to risk him seeing them.

My desire to pay Jodi back lingered beneath the surface, as if waiting for the moment I let my guard down. When would this be over, the battle of the new me against old habits? Would I ever feel like I was making headway?

"In all likelihood, no." Amy lowered the laundry basket of clean linens to the couch. "But someday you'll face a difficult situation and realize that not so long ago, you might have handled it poorly, yet you're no longer tempted to act that way. Then you'll know you've made progress."

I helped myself to a washcloth and folded it. "I wish it could be more like this. You can see ahead of time how much work there is to do, you know you're finished when the basket's empty, and you know you did a good job if it all stacks neatly in the closet."

Amy smiled. "Ah, but of course if we really knew how much work it'd be to change ourselves, we'd be too overwhelmed to get started."

I sighed. How true that felt. It seemed any progress I made only revealed more things needing work.

Amy's hand rested on my shoulder, and I looked up at her. "Don't be discouraged, Skylar. You're doing great."

For possibly the thousandth time, I wished she was my mother.

Cameron burst into the room. "Skylar, you said five minutes!"

"I know, I'm coming."

He tapped his foot as I smoothed away the wrinkles of a kitchen towel.

"Go on," Amy said, taking the towel from me. "I'm sure Connor's waiting on you too."

I glanced at the basket full of tangled towels and washcloths. Did Amy ever get breaks? My mom didn't seem to do half the housework Amy did, yet she was in constant need of time away. "You sure?"

"This'll take me no time at all." She shooed me off the couch. "Go be young."

Cameron snatched my hand and dragged me through the living room. "It's so cool," he said, stomping up the stairs. "The painter let me help. I did one of the stars, but I betcha can't tell which one because it looks just like his."

Since I'd seen his room last week, it had been completely transformed. No more plain blue walls, mismatched furniture, or ragged carpeting. Now painted furniture from—I'd bet—Pottery Barn Kids took its place. Three of his walls were painted dark with yellowish stars. The fourth wall, empty of furniture, had a large moon mural on it, as if you stood on its surface.

I made a big show of my admiration. "Wow, Cameron. This is the coolest room I've ever seen."

He hopped from one foot to another. "Guess which star I did. Guess which one."

"I don't know." I looked the walls up and down. "I can't tell."

"Connor, she can't tell either!" Cameron cried, and I turned to find Connor standing in the doorway. "I think I'm going to be a painter."

Connor smiled at his brother, then looked back to me. "Sorry, buddy, but I've got to steal Skylar. We have to study."

Cameron made a face. "Last time you said that, I saw you guys kissing."

I flushed, but Connor laughed. "We have a test tomorrow. We really do have to study."

Cameron launched into a song about K-I-S-S-I-N-G. As we headed down the hall toward Connor's room, Amy hollered up the stairs, "Stop that right now, Cameron Michael!"

Connor rolled his eyes. "Aren't little brothers the best?"

"No worse than my grumpy, withdrawn little sister."

"Still?" Connor grabbed his textbook and took the beanbag chair, leaving me the desk. "I thought she'd snap out of it by now."

Ever since her showdown with Lance last week, Abbie had been a recluse. A snippy recluse.

"What do you think it is?" Connor asked. "Just being freaked out about the baby?"

"I don't know." I drew my knees to my chest. "But it's weird because for a while we were so close, and now there's like this great big wall between us. And I don't even know how it happened."

"You're still close. It just goes in phases sometimes." He nodded at the wall dividing his room from Chris's. "We're like that too."

I sighed. Tons of things needed to be done—stocking the nursery, birthing classes, registering at the hospital—but Abbie didn't seem interested in any of them. And whenever I mentioned any of this to her, she told me to back off.

"If I knew you'd take care of things, I wouldn't have to constantly bug you about it," I'd told her yesterday.

"Just leave me alone," Abbie said as she stormed away. "You're my sister, not my mom." She slammed her bedroom door, leaving me alone to ponder various retorts.

Abbie hadn't been too affected by our fighting. Twenty minutes later, I'd heard her snoring.

"There's so much that needs to be done," I said to Connor. "I'm trying to figure out a way to do it all, but Abbie keeps backing away from me."

"March 10 is still a ways away."

I blinked at him. "Connor, today's the *twenty-eighth*. We've got six weeks until her due date, and we don't have a crib or diapers or clothes . . ." I trailed off as Connor covered my hands with his.

"It'll all get done. And I'll do whatever I can to help."

"Something about this feels wrong. She shouldn't be acting like this."

"She shouldn't be in this situation to begin with. *That's* why it seems like she's acting weird."

I wanted to believe Connor was right, that this gnawing fear in my belly was an overreaction. But when I returned home a couple hours later, I knew he'd been wrong. That things were far from okay.

Mom's Lexus sat in the driveway.

I found Mom and Abbie seated at the kitchen table.

"No cookies today?" I asked in a dry voice from the doorway.

Mom's mouth twitched into her normal, cool smile. "Hi. We didn't think you'd be home this early."

I glanced at Abbie, who stared into a steaming mug of something. The kitchen reeked of coffee. Hopefully Mom thought to make decaf for Abbie.

"What's going on?" I asked, lowering my backpack to the floor.

"You want coffee?"

"I hate coffee."

Mom nodded. "Do you want to join us?"

"Is it, like, a private club or something?"

Her mouth pressed into a line. "Don't be snotty, Skylar."

I plopped into the farthest chair from them, at the head of the long, oval table. My sister still wouldn't look at me.

"What are you doing here?" I asked Mom.

"This is still my house."

"You know what I mean."

Mom reached for the stainless steel carafe and refilled her cup, then Abbie's. "I'm here to talk to your dad about Hawaii. About making this as simple and easy a transition as possible."

Abbie looked at me. Already my head ached from grinding my teeth.

"And what's your story?" I asked.

She hesitated. "Please don't be mad—"

"Abbie, you *can't* go. You're having a baby—"

"Stop saying that! You think I don't know I'm having a baby?" She raked her hands through her hair and took several deep breaths. "I can't stay at school much longer anyway, so I might as well drop out now. And Mom explained the situation to the insurance company, so it won't be a problem for me to switch doctors."

"Explained the situation," I repeated in a flat voice. I cut my gaze to Mom. "I'd love to hear that."

"Skylar, you know the situation," Mom said, well measured as always. "I let you make your choice, and now you should let Abbie make hers."

Had I really been stupid enough to dream this was over?

That Mom wouldn't try to talk Abbie into going? That Abbie wouldn't feel swayed to go?

Abbie splayed her hands on the table. "I have a chance to start over. Everybody needs a fresh start."

I bit back a laugh. Those words had echoed in my head since Mom had said them to me at Starbucks. What an alluring idea, a fresh start. Reinventing yourself. Not being accountable for past mistakes.

Only now I saw it as a chicken's way out.

"You could come with us," Abbie said. "No more Jodi. Wouldn't it be great?"

I ignored this and focused on Mom. "So you're really going to Hawaii?"

"I told you I was."

"You also said you were here to stay, so I don't exactly trust you."

"He cheated on her. Did you know that, Skylar?" Abbie turned to Mom. "Did you tell her?"

Mom's gaze didn't leave my face as she answered Abbie. "Your sister thinks I'm overreacting."

"Overreacting?" Abbie gaped at me. "Remember how you felt when Eli cheated on *you*?"

"Mom and Dad aren't in high school."

She rolled her eyes. "See what I mean?" she said to Mom, her voice brimming with bitterness.

"What?" I asked, wary.

"You have no compassion anymore," Abbie said. "It's like you're so much better than everyone else."

My jaw dropped. She couldn't have said anything more hurtful. "That isn't true." *Please, God, don't let that be true.*

"It *is* true! You were crushed when Eli cheated on you,

137

and you didn't even like him most of the time you dated. But it's not okay for Mom to be hurt by what Dad did?"

Mom looked confused. "When did you date Eli?"

No time for that now. To Abbie, I said, "I'm not saying Mom shouldn't be hurt—"

"You hound me about all this stuff I need to get done, about how you think I should be living my life. Like you're some kind of expert. You know, I wouldn't even be pregnant if it weren't for you."

"Abbie . . ." I couldn't think of anything to say. I longed for her to take it back.

Tears streaked Abbie's face. "We can't all be like you, Skylar. You've always been so beautiful and perfect. You suck up all the oxygen in the room, never leaving anything for me."

"That's not true—"

"Who are you to say whether or not it's true?" Abbie's chair grated across the tile as she stood. "Do you know what it's like to be plain and boring while your sister's some exotic beauty?"

"How can you say that?" I asked, assessing her shiny auburn hair, her seemingly pore-free skin.

"You think you're so superior, but one of these days something bad is going to happen to you"—Abbie jabbed at her stomach—"and everyone will know what a fraud you really are." Abbie marched out of the room. Mom and I watched her go.

Mom winced at the sound of Abbie's bedroom door slamming. "She doesn't mean a lot of that. She's just moody."

"But . . ." I pushed back in my chair, frustrated. Mom and Abbie had the gift of starting an argument, then leaving before you could finish it. "Is it so horrible that I've been trying to talk her into childbirth classes? Into buying diapers before we bring home the baby?"

"Of course not."

"And I don't think I'm better than everyone else," I muttered.

Or did I? It had only been a few weeks since Connor harped at me for the same thing.

Mom sipped at her coffee. "So, you dated Eli?"

"Yeah."

"You just blatantly disregarded our rules?" She wagged her head. "What a horrible example to set for your sister."

I couldn't help laughing. "Do you also blame me for Abbie getting pregnant, or is that just her?"

Mom's mouth pursed. "The responsibility for that lies with Abbie and Lance alone."

I released the breath I didn't realize I'd been holding. She'd said what I needed to hear, and now maybe I could offer her something. "It's not that I don't understand why you're angry with Dad," I said in a soft voice. "I just wish you'd keep working on it."

Mom snorted, the most undignified sound I'd ever heard from her. "Keep working on it. Right."

"Why don't you go back to counseling? It seemed like you guys were making progress."

Her expression hardened. "This isn't open for discussion. I'm not taking advice from my teenage daughter."

"Maybe you should," Dad said from the doorway. Both Mom and I jumped. "She's pretty smart."

How long had he been standing there? With his gaze still on Mom, Dad said, "Skylar, please excuse us."

The screech of my chair sounded extra loud in the tense quiet. Mom's and Dad's gazes remained locked on each other, reminding me of those Discovery Channel shows about face-offs between animals.

I hustled out of the room and upstairs, not wanting to get any more involved in the battle. Outside my room, I paused and looked toward Abbie's closed bedroom door. It didn't completely muffle her crying. I tiptoed closer, my hand hesitating on the doorknob.

I thought of earlier, of her venomous words.

I withdrew my hand and retreated to my own room. Why bother helping her when she didn't appreciate it?

I attempted a variety of activities—studying for American History, cleaning out my closet, sewing—before I finally gave up and called Connor. He didn't answer his cell, so I called his house line, aggravated that I'd become one of those girls I'd always pitied, the ones who called their boyfriends in the tiniest of crises. Of course, this wasn't a "tiny" crisis. I didn't know what this was, really.

Curtis answered with a chirpy, "Hello, Ross redi-sense."

"Hi, Curtis, it's Skylar. Is Connor—"

"Skylar!" he cried with the enthusiasm that appeared endless with five-year-olds. "Mom said you were here earlier. I was at Tae Kwon Do. I learned how to do a front snap kick and a forearm block and—"

"Curtis?" Amy said in the background. "Don't forget to ask who she's calling for. Remember how we practiced?"

"Oh, right." Curtis took on a rehearsed voice. "Who would you like to speak with?"

I grinned. I was so not a kid person, but it was impossible not to adore Curtis. "Is Connor there?"

"He is, but . . . hey, Mom? What do I say if he's here but doesn't want to talk?"

"Did Connor say he didn't want to talk?" I could hear Amy's frown through the phone.

"Yeah. I was in his room showing him my new moves when that girl showed up. And he said, 'If Skylar calls, I can't talk.'"

Could you actually feel a coronary? If symptoms included a faltering heartbeat, a loud whooshing in the ears, and the mind focusing on one thought and one thought only—*IS IT JODI??*—then I'd swear I just had one.

"Is it Jodi, Curtis?" I asked as Amy said, "Give me the phone, Curtis."

"What'd I do?" he whimpered.

"Nothing, I just want to speak to Skylar," Amy said, her voice considerably softer. She came on the line. "Hi, sweetie."

My entire mouth had gone dry. "Is Jodi there?"

She hesitated long enough that I knew before she confirmed it. "Yes. I'm sorry to be the one to tell you. I thought you knew she came over."

"*Came* over?" I repeated. "As in, this happens often?"

Amy groaned. "You should talk to Connor about this. I didn't mean to get involved, but I could tell I hadn't trained Curtis for what was going on."

What was going on?

"I'll be right over."

I hung up before Amy responded, then just sat there. How could Connor do this to me? Of course, he'd be able to twist this around and justify it. He'd leave me feeling suddenly stupid for being mad. The pitfalls of dating someone smarter. It would probably be like the last time I drove over there to yell at him—I wound up angry with myself. But I didn't care. I had to go.

I thundered down the stairs, snippets of our recent conversations running through my head. I'd told him to be careful with her. He knew she made me nervous, that his relationship with her wasn't a compromise issue. If he wanted to be nice to her, fine, but he shouldn't be inviting her over to his place. Repeatedly. And telling his baby brother to lie to me.

"Skylar!"

With my right hand halfway to the door to the garage, I turned to face my dad. He and Mom sat at the kitchen table, one chair between them. "What?"

"Where are you going?"

"Connor's."

"Well, it's gonna have to wait. Your mother and I have something to discuss with you girls."

"It can't wait." I took a breath to explain but didn't know how to tell my father that a sleazy, manipulative girl had wormed her way into my boyfriend's house in an attempt to steal him.

"It can wait," Dad said as he strode to the base of the stairs. "Abbie? Will you come down here, please?"

Nothing.

"It'll take me less than five minutes," I pleaded. Two minutes to drive to Connor's, two minutes to drive back, and thirty seconds to inform him we were over. That's all it had taken for me to end things with Eli when I'd caught him cheating with Jodi. Okay, I hadn't *caught* them, but I'd overheard them talking about what happened between them the night of homecoming.

Dad turned on his no-nonsense voice. "Sit down." Up the stairs, he boomed, "Abigail Marie? Can you hear me?"

I appealed to Mom. Surely as a woman . . . "I *have* to go."

But she looked even sterner than Dad. "Your father said to sit."

"So, suddenly you're on the same team?"

"Watch it, young lady," Dad said. "Abbie?"

"I hope you two know"—I yanked a chair out from the table—"you're making a mess of my life."

"Well, what's new?" Dad said, then jogged upstairs.

I fidgeted as my brain burned with questions about Connor and Jodi. How long had this been going on? Before Eli and Jodi broke up? Before he knew she liked him? There had to be a good explanation. Connor wouldn't sneak around behind my back. I knew him.

Didn't I?

Dad returned downstairs with a puffy-faced, sulking Abbie. She collapsed into a chair without looking at me.

Dad settled into his seat and clasped his hands on the table. "Well, girls, your mom and I have been talking. She's filled me in on her plans to move to Hawaii, and she says she's talked to both you girls about it."

He looked to us for confirmation. We nodded.

"Okay." Sadness flickered on his face, replaced quickly by a look of stony resolve. "So at the end of the school year, you'll both move out there."

15

"What?" Abbie and I said simultaneously.

"I'm not moving to Hawaii," I said.

"And I'm moving before the baby comes."

Mom nodded at Abbie. "I know we talked about that, but as your dad and I discussed it, it made less and less sense. You can have the baby here with your doctor, in that nice new hospital. That way all your friends will be close by."

"I don't *want* my friends close by," Abbie growled. "That's why I'm moving."

I forced a laugh. "Yes, run away. That'll solve everything."

Abbie glared at me but didn't respond.

"Abbie, I know things are really difficult for you at school," Dad said, "but you don't want to be moving this late in your pregnancy. Who knows how long it'll take for your mom to find a house, and you want to be settled before you bring the baby home."

It amazed me how calmly he discussed this. His wife— the love of his life, he claimed—buying a house far, far away and taking his girls and granddaughter with her.

I narrowed my eyes. "What do you get out of this?"

Dad glanced at me. "Pardon?"

"I thought you wanted us to be a family. Now you're telling Abbie and me to move?"

He frowned. "This is about what I think—what *we* think—is best for you girls."

"Well, I'm not going." I leaned back in my chair and crossed my arms.

"You don't want to be there for your sister and her baby?" Mom asked.

"Ha!" I let the chair fall onto all four legs. "I'm not the one who keeps running off and then shows back up whenever she feels like it. I'm taking her to doctor appointments, reminding her the baby's going to need diapers one of these days—"

"Stop it," Abbie snapped. "Let Skylar stay if she wants to."

Mom hesitated. She glanced at Dad, but he stared into his coffee cup. "Skylar, I really think you should come. At least for the summer."

I pushed back in my chair and let it fall again because I knew Mom hated it. She said it wore out the furniture. She'd always worried about wearing out furniture, which seemed strange since we never kept anything longer than a couple years.

"I'm not going. I'm eighteen, and I'm not going."

Dad looked at me. "Are you sure, honey? Maybe it'd be good for you to get away. At least for the summer. You've had a rough year."

Abbie sneered. "Yeah. *Skylar's* had a rough year."

I ignored her and said to Dad, "I'm not leaving you here alone."

"Your father wants you to go, Skylar," Mom said.

But Mom wasn't looking at Dad. She didn't see the faint relief in his smile.

This all confused me. Why would Dad give up and let Mom move to Hawaii? Did she have, like, embarrassing pictures of him? Evidence of tax evasion? I just didn't buy that he thought it was best for us. In what universe would it be best?

As we sat there for over an hour making plans, I still couldn't figure it out.

"Who's hungry?" Mom asked, reaching for the phone. "Let's order takeout."

I glanced at the clock. A little after nine. "Isn't it kinda late?"

"Oh, it doesn't matter," Mom said as she scrolled through the list of numbers saved on our phone, mostly restaurants. "I'll be staying here until I move."

That wasn't what I'd meant. I'd meant all of Mom's favorite restaurants would be closed by now.

"You'll be staying here?" I repeated. That sure cleared things up. I stared at Dad, but he wouldn't meet my eye line.

"Your father and I discussed it, and it only makes sense. How does pizza sound to everyone? I think everywhere good is closed."

Dad had once told me he'd stop at nothing to be with the person he loved. Did that include gambling that if she stayed here—in the nice, comfy house where she didn't have to worry about working—she might never leave for Hawaii?

"I'd like to place an order for delivery," Mom said into the phone.

Dad finally looked at me. "Didn't you have something you needed to do at the Rosses'?"

My boyfriend lying to me—right.

I pushed back from the table, my legs aching from sitting in the same position for so long. "I'll be back soon."

"Can I come?" Abbie asked.

I hesitated. I didn't want anyone witnessing what was about to go down, but it'd been awhile since Abbie had looked at me without narrowing her eyes. And some company might be nice. Especially for the drive home.

I shrugged. "Whatever."

Mom hung up the phone. "Pizza will be here in thirty."

"We'll be back in plenty of time." I grabbed my keys off the kitchen counter and left through the garage door. In the car, I said, "No dillydallying. I don't plan on staying long."

"Yeah, I gathered. What's going on?"

"Nothing." If she thought I'd tell her after the betrayal that had just happened . . .

Abbie sighed. "I'm sorry about earlier. About the things I said. I can be a hothead, you know. And my hormones are crazy these days."

"That's not an excuse."

"I know, I just . . ." Abbie sighed and leaned back in her seat. "You're really difficult to like sometimes. You're so—"

"Don't say *perfect*."

She gazed out the window, at the lit-up houses we'd passed hundreds of times before. "I need to get away from here. Start over."

I said nothing, just ached with jealousy.

At the Ross house, Abbie knocked on the door. It seemed extra quiet inside. I couldn't even hear Cevin yapping.

The delay in confronting Connor had worn off some of the anger, replacing it with sadness. I hoped I wouldn't cry. Was it wrong to hope *he* would?

Connor answered the door wearing the same clothes as when I'd left a few hours before. Funny how he looked totally different to me.

He didn't say hello or invite us in. He just looked at me and I looked back, suddenly so overwhelmed with hurt I couldn't think of a thing to say.

Abbie's gaze flitted between us. "I'm gonna go find Chris." She slipped past Connor.

Connor pulled the door shut behind him as he stepped outside. I sat on the front step, then he joined me.

We'd never spent so long together without talking. So much for quick and painless. This breakup would be long, drawn-out torture.

"I don't even know where to begin." Connor looked at me with big, beautiful eyes. "It's not what you think, Skylar."

I took a shaky breath. "It's not? Because I'm not even really sure what I think."

"You think I'm falling for her."

"Yeah." It came out as a whisper.

"But I'm not. I love *you*. Nothing's changing that."

"Then why's she coming over? Why'd you tell Curtis to lie to me?"

"I knew how it'd look. I knew you'd be mad." He scuffed the sole of his shoe along the stone steps. "I should've told you. I was stupid."

My voice returned to a normal volume. "Tell me now."

Connor sighed. "Jodi said she wanted to talk about the Bible—"

I huffed.

He sighed again and continued. "She said she felt kinda dumb at youth group because everyone seemed to know so much more than she did. She asked if she could come over to the house, like, twice a week so I could help her. That's all that happened. I'm so sorry I didn't tell you."

"Do you know what it was like to hear about it from Curtis?" I glared at him. He looked nervous. I couldn't remember the last time I'd seen Connor nervous. "To hear how sorry your mom felt for me?"

"I was being really stupid. Believe me, both my parents have beat that into me tonight. Jodi won't be coming over anymore."

"Good."

"I just . . ." He tapped his toes a couple times. "I just wanted to help her. She needs a nice guy in her life."

"God will send her someone else."

"I hope so. I just—"

"I don't care what you 'just,'" I snapped. "It's not negotiable. You continuing to hang out with her isn't an option if you want to be with me. Jodi's the end of us. Period."

Connor nodded and stared at his grungy sneakers.

I turned away and looked at the yard, at the glowing solar lights lining the walkway. If only the right path could always be so well-lit and obvious.

"What are you thinking about?" This time Connor waited for me to answer instead of giving his own theory.

But I didn't want to voice my thoughts.

Of Jodi and Connor—did he think she was prettier than me?

About Kapaa. It was probably nice and warm there.

But mostly I wondered if this thing I was attempting—fitting my new self into my old life—was really worth it.

"Nothing important," I said to Connor.

At least temporarily, his name had been scratched off the short list of people I trusted.

16

I'm wearing that bathing suit again, the black-and-white one.

This time there isn't a palm tree or speck of golden sand in sight. Instead, I'm on our front lawn. And on the front lawn is my bedroom. Not the walls, but everything else— my bed, my dresser, my desk—arranged exactly the same. As if I've been turned out of my own house. As if I'm being told to move on.

I jolted awake, relieved to find myself inside the house and dressed in flannel pj's. I took several gulps of air and found my mouth dry like cotton.

Even though I was in my warmest pajamas, winter's chill surrounded me as I pulled back the blankets and climbed out of bed. I tiptoed out of my room and down the hall, past Mom and Dad's closed bedroom doors. Who slept in there now, Mom or Dad? I'd guess Mom. It seemed unfair that every time she decided to come home, Dad got kicked out of his own room.

When I saw a faint glow coming from the kitchen, I hesitated at the bottom of the steps. I didn't hear anyone. Someone must've left on a light.

I rounded the corner to discover it wasn't a kitchen light

but Dad's office lamp. He knelt beside his desk, his head bowed.

I stepped backward—I'd get a drink from my bathroom sink—but my elbow smacked the refrigerator door handle. "Ouch!"

Dad's head snapped up, and I covered my mouth. "Sorry," I said. "I just came down for a drink. I didn't mean to interrupt you."

He shook his head and used the desk to pull himself up. Boy, he looked old. Of course it was three in the morning, he still wore his rumpled work clothes, and it had been a couple days since he'd shaved.

"I'm happy to have the interruption." Dad gestured to the floor where he'd been. "This praying stuff . . . I don't know how good I am at it."

"Mom's here, isn't she?" I said. "That's something."

"Yeah, it's something." Dad scratched his head. His hair stuck out in crazy directions. I'd never seen him so disheveled.

"Can I get you something?" I asked. "Coffee? Tea? A comb?"

Dad smoothed his hair and gave me a bland smile. "Frightful, I'm sure."

"You wanna talk?"

He shook his head. "You've been in the middle too much, Skylar. I'm sorry. I don't want to do that to you anymore."

I wouldn't have minded listening to him, but it was nice for him to acknowledge the tough position he and Mom had put me in.

"So what are you doing awake?" Dad asked.

"I'm thirsty."

"That's right. You said that. Should I make us some tea?"

I didn't know if I liked tea any better than coffee, but the idea of holding a warm, steamy mug sounded comforting. "Sure."

While I pulled two mugs from the cabinet, Dad filled the teapot and started the gas burner. Then we stood there, watching the flicker of the blue flame in the darkened kitchen.

"We probably shouldn't do this," Dad said. "You know what they say about a watched pot."

"Can I ask a question about you and Mom?"

"Sure."

"You're hoping she doesn't go to Hawaii, right?"

Dad continued to stare at the stove, an amused smile on his face. "Am I that transparent?"

"Back in October you told me we were similar, that we'd both do whatever it took to be with the person we loved. It seemed strange for you to give up now." I studied his profile. "You know, you could lose everything. Mom, Abbie, the baby."

"Or I could end up with it all." Dad fit his arm around my shoulder, and I leaned against him. "You have no idea what a comfort it is to know I'll have you no matter what your mom ultimately decides."

My heart sputtered. With the weirdness of Connor and Jodi, Hawaii looked pretty good right now. I thought of earlier on Connor's porch step, of how sorry he said he felt. But was it enough to keep it from happening again?

"In your experience with Mom," I said slowly, "has it been worth it?"

"Has what been worth it?"

"Sticking around. Waiting for her to realize she's being stupid and should come home."

The corners of his mouth turned down. "Yes. Although this time, *I* was stupid." Dad shook his head as if disgusted. "An affair is an ugly, nasty business, Skylar. Even if your mom chooses to stay, it's a long, tough road ahead for both of us."

I sighed. "I know. But it'd be so nice if you could talk her into it."

"We have to be careful with deception," Dad said. "If we have to deceive to keep something, it probably wasn't really ours to begin with."

I'd set my alarm super early, planning to get ready and yank Abbie off to school before Connor and Chris pulled into our drive. After I returned to bed from my conversation with Dad, I lay awake a long time. So long, I imagined the alarm would be unnecessary.

And then, the next thing I knew, Abbie stood over my bed, shaking me. "Skylar, the guys are here."

I blinked at her, my eyes aching like overused muscles. "What time is it?"

"7:30." She shut off my radio and waddled out of the room. "Hurry up."

"You know, you could've woken me up sooner!" I called as she shut my door. If Abbie answered, I didn't hear it.

Somehow I made it downstairs by 7:40—teeth and hair brushed, outfit decent, and even a little makeup. Pretty darn impressive.

"Sorry," I said, breathless as I slid into my normal spot in the passenger's seat. "Thanks for waiting."

Connor put the car in reverse. "No worries."

"Yeah, I'm sure my first period teacher will understand," Abbie said, her voice pure sarcasm.

"You guys could've gone without me. I told you to tell Connor that."

"He wouldn't leave Queen Skylar behind."

Connor flashed an irritated look her way, something I'd never seen him do. She grunted but didn't say anything else.

"So, you overslept?" Connor asked.

"Yep."

He glanced at me, but I kept my focus on the road. Where his should've been. "You look tired."

"Because I am."

"Are your pants new?"

I drew my knees to my chest and wrapped my arms around them. "Uh-huh."

"I like them."

Oh, come on. Connor never commented on my clothes except when ridiculing me. I didn't answer.

In the backseat, Chris and Abbie were quiet as well. Recently they'd been a little chattier, a little more comfortable with each other. Apparently the effects of last night lingered for them as well. Abbie had told Chris about Hawaii. I assumed this meant Connor knew by now, and the only reason he hadn't brought it up was we'd yet to be alone.

I assumed correctly.

At school, as we split off from our siblings, Connor said,

"So Chris told me about your mom and Abbie moving. I'm really sorry."

I shrugged. "Yeah, well."

"They're staying at the house until they move?"

"Looks like it."

"That'll be kinda weird."

"Yeah."

Connor wove his fingers through mine. "Whenever you're ready to talk about it, just let me know."

I snorted. "I tried last night. You were preoccupied."

He sighed and released my lifeless fingers. "I know, Skylar."

"No, you don't." I spun my combination into my locker, anxious to open the door and put space between us. "If you 'knew,' then you wouldn't be chatting with me like everything is fine."

"I know everything's not fine." Connor leaned against Eli's closed locker. "I know it's going to take time, but I'm really not sure how to act until then."

The black anger surging through me felt so familiar. Like the last time Jodi had involved herself in my relationship. I'd recovered from Eli's damage—hadn't I?—and surely I could do it again.

I took a few wobbly breaths. "I just don't trust you right now."

"I know, and I understand, but—"

"Hey, you two." Jodi sauntered down the hall toward her locker. "Can you believe how cold it is outside?"

I looked at her.

I hadn't *really* looked at Jodi in a long time. She was beautiful, she really was. Especially when she wore her strawberry blonde hair up in a ponytail. It showcased her long cheekbones and her round, dark eyes. The same round, dark eyes Connor had been looking into as he helped her with Bible comprehension. How could he not feel anything for her? I'd gamble my Juicy jeans that she'd been saying all the right words, pulling out her most subtle flirting moves. And I'd seen firsthand what kind of damage she could do.

After passing Connor, Jodi winked at me.

I wished I'd stayed on the phone longer with Curtis the night before and let him detail all his Tae Kwon Do moves.

With a slam of my locker door, I charged out of there.

How could Jodi be like this? We'd bonded over caramel pretzel crunch ice cream and the thrills of our first cars. What was it about guys, about revenge, that trumped our years of friendship?

Connor caught up to me. I expected him to say something about being nice to Jodi, about how it hadn't been necessary to storm out of there.

"I just don't want to be around her right now," I said before he could talk.

"You have nothing to apologize for."

I slowed my pace. "Yeah?"

"Yeah."

I smiled a little. He did too. The first tentative steps toward normality.

17

Heather flung open her front door. "I'm going to Uganda!"

I blinked at her through the flakes of snow falling between us.

"You're letting in cold air, c'mon." Heather grabbed my sewing basket as I stepped inside the house.

"You're going to Uganda?" I repeated, dropping my fabric onto the already cluttered loveseat. "Like, Africa?"

"That's the one." Heather pranced around the corner into the kitchen. "You want coffee? I just made some."

I followed her. "Sure." I'd had coffee too many times at Heather's to tell her now that I didn't like it.

She opened a blue foil package. "It's a winter blend. Smell it." She waved it beneath my nose. "Doesn't it smell wonderful?"

It smelled better than regular coffee, I'd give her that. *Wonderful* wasn't exactly the word that came to mind.

"When are you going to Africa?"

"Tuesday. Can you believe it? I have so much to do. I've been too excited to sleep." Heather bounded to the cupboard where she kept mugs. "I'm using up all my paid vacation and had to beg a couple girls to cover some shifts, but I don't care. I mean, this is the whole reason I became a nurse, so I could do this kind of stuff. Cream?"

"Sure."

She twirled on her way to the fridge. Actually twirled. I'd rarely been so happy that I danced.

"You wanna know how I wound up going?"

I could tell by the gleam in her eye that this involved a guy.

Sure enough, Brent Sanders, the new NICU doctor she'd told me about. As we worked, Heather told me how one of the nurses on the Uganda team had to back out last minute, and Brent thought Heather might like to go.

"Oh, Skylar, he's so . . . so . . . dreamy." Heather giggled, and momentarily *I* felt like the adult in the room. "That sounds like something my mom would say, but it's the only word I can think of. He took me out to dinner last night. We talked and talked and talked."

I pasted on a smile. "That's great. I'm really happy for you."

Heather settled herself down. "I know I sound like an idiot, and I know it's still early, but I just can't help it. I've never felt this way about a guy."

"It's about time you met someone. You deserve it." I resumed my sewing. Had I sounded sincere? Of course, I really *was* happy for Heather; it had just been a rough week. I'd anticipated coming over and her making it all better. And now she planned to leave for nearly three weeks.

Heather grinned at my project. "Is that for Abbie?"

I nodded. "I can hardly get her interested in shopping for the baby. I figured I could at least make some bedding."

"I love this." Heather picked up a swatch of fabric, the pink corduroy. For the bumper, I'd selected pink corduroy, tan corduroy, and an off-white pattern with rosebuds. Abbie dug the whole shabby chic look.

"You know, I have some ribbon that would be perfect with this. It's in the extra room." Heather abandoned cutting her curtains, which she'd been too bouncy to pay much attention to anyway, and trotted off down the hallway. I sighed and followed.

I leaned against the doorway and watched as Heather carefully stepped around the crowded floor. "How do you find anything in here?"

"It's a bit disheveled, isn't it? I kept thinking I'd hang on to stuff because when I got a bigger house I'd want it, but now I've been here four years. Maybe I'll give all of it the heave-ho when I come back from Uganda."

She wrestled with the bottom drawer of a large bureau. "I know it's in here somewhere." She pulled out a large plastic box full of wires and unidentifiable odds and ends. "I really wish Jodi would join us. I thought she was interested."

"Yeah, I don't know." I occupied myself with all the pictures on the wall. "You know lots of people."

"A large family does that."

I leaned closer to one of Heather with her arms around Mickey and Minnie Mouse. "When did you go to Disney World?"

"Couple years ago with my sister and her kids. We had the best time."

I moved down the line—birthday parties, fancy dinners, Christmas morning—then froze at Aaron's face grinning back at me from a wedding photo.

"Found it!" Heather declared, and I jumped. She giggled. "Did I startle you?"

"Kinda." I looked back to the picture of Aaron. Surely I was mistaken . . . No. I'd recognize that face anywhere. "This is Aaron Robinson, isn't it?" I worked hard to keep my voice casual.

Heather gave me a funny look. "You know Aaron?"

I shrugged. "We used to run in the same circle."

"Huh." She crossed the room and examined the photo as well, a spool of ribbon dangling from one hand. "Do you know Lane?"

I shook my head.

"That's my sister." She pointed to the girl sitting next to him in a bridesmaid dress, fair and beautiful like Heather. "Lane and Aaron dated for . . . a year, I guess. I'm surprised you don't know her."

"I didn't know Aaron real well." Strange. He'd catapulted this season of my life, this weird in-between place, yet I *didn't* know him. Where did he live? Who were his parents? Did he have brothers and sisters? "I just met him last summer. We have mutual friends."

"Hmm." Heather looked back at the picture, her expression dim. "I'm sure he's a nice guy, but he really broke my sister's heart."

"He's *not* a nice guy," I said, and the venom in my voice surprised both of us.

Her eyes widened. "No?"

I needed to chill. "From what I hear."

"He was really horrible to Lane." Heather turned back to the picture. She seemed forlorn. "My sister is wonderful, but she's a real people pleaser. She let him walk all over her." Heather sighed. "Praise God he cheated on her, because otherwise she probably would've followed him to school in Florida."

"He cheated on her?" My mouth felt desert dry.

"Yeah. He was a partier, and I guess some friend of Lane's saw him take another girl into a bedroom." Heather shuddered. "So creepy."

"Yeah. Creepy."

So, okay, I didn't have proof that her friend saw me and Aaron at Jodi's party. There'd been lots of parties last summer. Still . . .

Heather's voice brightened. "But like I said, praise God it happened, because Lane is much better off."

How funny. Through a slimy guy and a sleazy night, it appeared God freed two unrelated, very lost girls.

"Nursing?" Mom blinked at me. "What about fashion?"

I feigned cluelessness. "What do you mean?"

"What do I mean?" Mom chuckled. "You've *always* talked about going into fashion or design or whatever they call it these days."

"Actually, *I* never talked about it." I picked around my plate. "Everyone else just said it's what I should do."

"For good reason," Mom said. "It's the only thing you've ever done well."

Gee, thanks, Mom.

"But majors are easy enough to change," Dad said. "I say you give nursing a try. If you get in there and don't like it, you can always switch."

"Figures that'd be your advice," Mom muttered.

"What's that, Teri?" Dad asked, his smile sweet.

Abbie met my gaze across the table as the conversation

ceased to be about my college plans. That's how it went these days when we were all together. Everything turned into snide comments between Mom and Dad, a veiled tug-of-war.

Mom bared her teeth. "Shouldn't we be encouraging our daughters to stick with something, even if it's hard? Not to just run off and do whatever they want, but to be responsible for choices?"

"Yes." Dad gave her a hard look. "I think that's exactly what we should be teaching them."

"Chris asked me to Sweetheart."

If Abbie blurted it to stop the arguing, it worked. Both Mom and Dad abandoned their battle and turned to her. Even my eyes widened. She hadn't told me that. Of course, we weren't telling each other very much these days.

"No," Mom said in a flat voice.

"Why not?" Abbie asked.

She looked at Abbie's round stomach. "Do I really have to explain?"

Abbie laughed, sounding as carefree as the old Abbie. "It's just a dance. My feet will be too swollen to do anything anyway. We'll probably just sit there on the bleachers and talk."

"No," Mom said again. She looked to Dad, as if expecting him to back her. "Paul?"

Dad shrugged. "What's the worst that can happen?"

Mom's left eye twitched. "The house rule is no dating until college."

"Come on, Mom," I said. "I have a boyfriend, and Abbie's eight months pregnant."

"Skylar, no sassing your mother," Dad said.

I rolled my eyes. I guess we could share however many three a.m. pots of tea, but when it came down to it, he was on Mom's side.

Mom fixed Dad with a stony face. "Maybe if you'd do better at showing a united front, the girls wouldn't think it's okay to talk back."

"Oh, please." Dad wiped his mouth, possibly to cover his amused smile. Little irritated Mom more than when Dad wouldn't stop grinning during a fight. "What kind of a united front do you plan to have when you're living in Hawaii and I'm here?"

"That was a choice you made."

"That I made?" Dad laughed. "If it were up to me, we'd still be in counseling."

"If you were so concerned with our marriage, maybe you—"

Abbie's chair grated against the tile. She stood as gracefully as she could.

"Sit down, Abigail. We're having a family dinner," Dad said.

Abbie sneered. "This isn't a family," she said, and she stalked from the room.

Her words sent a shiver through me. With Mom and Abbie in Hawaii, and Dad and me here, what *did* that make the four of us?

18

"Shouldn't Abbie be doing this?" Connor cast a nervous glance at the other shoppers. I didn't blame him. We looked a little weird, the two of us roaming the aisles of Babies R Us.

"Don't get me started." With one hand, I clutched a six-pack of cloth diapers. With the other, I held open Abbie's pregnancy book. "It says she needs twelve of these. Why does she need twelve?"

"Beats me." Connor fiddled with a plastic dolphin that squirted water. "Get her one of these. These are awesome."

Why had I thought bringing Connor would be helpful? He'd reverted to being a little kid, constantly distracted by toys and worthless items. I may as well have brought Cameron or Curtis for support. Chris—he'd have been the smart choice. At least he'd have taken this seriously.

"Uh-oh." Connor stashed the toy. "I can tell by your face I'm about to get in trouble." He pressed a fingertip to the bridge of my nose, where it had wrinkled. He grinned. "I'll be good, I swear."

I wasn't in the mood to find him charming. I waved the questionable package of cloth diapers. "What do you think?"

"I don't know." He took them from me, turned them over. "What are they for, anyway? Won't she use Pampers or whatever?"

"I guess they're good for stuff like spit-up." I shrugged. "I don't know. I'm just doing what the book says. The book says twelve."

"Then get both packs, but only open one. Then you can return it."

So maybe he wasn't completely worthless.

I tossed them in the cart, along with the bottles, sippy cups, hooded towels, and washcloths. It felt like we'd been here forever, yet we'd barely made a dent in the list. Babies apparently had lots of needs.

Connor returned to his position at the head of the cart. "What's next?"

"A bathtub." I looked around. "Where do you think those are?"

"Your house didn't come with a bathtub?"

I fixed him with a cross look. "A *baby* bathtub. It goes inside the regular tub—"

"I know what it is. I was just joking." He pointed ahead. "They're in that aisle. I saw them during the cloth diaper search." He forged ahead, and I walked beside him, my head still in the book.

"So what should we do after this?"

"After this?" I turned the list to him—we'd crossed off five items, and there were, oh, five million left. "There won't be an 'after this.' We're never going to leave this place."

"Well, we don't have to get it all today, do we? The baby's not coming today."

"The baby could come any day now." I picked up a tub

165

shaped like a duck. "We're about four weeks out. I packed our hospital bag last night."

Connor frowned. "Is it just me, or is Abbie doing squat?"

"This is how Abbie is. When a situation gets too emotionally heavy, she checks out."

"That should be fun with a baby."

I sighed. "I don't know what to do."

"Personally, I like the cow tub."

"I'm talking about Abbie."

"I know." He crouched beside me. His hand warmed my back. "I love that you want to take care of your sister, I do, but you can't take *over* your sister. The baby is hers, and Abbie has to be responsible."

"I wish it were mine." I wiped away the tears suddenly dripping from my eyes. "I mean, not that I wish I was having a baby, but I wish I could have it instead of Abbie. She's too young for this. What's she going to do for money? How's she going to finish high school? What about—"

"Shh." Connor pulled me against him, although both of us were a bit wobbly, crouched there like frogs. "You don't have to figure that stuff out. Abbie does."

"It's all my fault." Oh gosh, I was going to have an emotional breakdown right here in the baby superstore. People really would think I was pregnant. "If I hadn't helped her sneak around with Lance, if I'd set a better example—"

"No." His hand clapped over my mouth. "You and Abbie made your own choices. Stop blaming yourself."

I sniffled. "You'd feel differently if it were Chris."

"Maybe." He smoothed my hair.

"You would. Of course, you'll never know because you're always a perfect example."

"Not always."

Even before he said anything else, I knew Jodi had entered our conversation. The shadows of last week's fight lingered, no matter how hard I worked to forgive. No matter how much he ignored her at school.

He glanced at me. "How are we doing?"

"Fine." I stood, leaving him there on the floor. I loaded the duck tub into the cart. "I think we've gotten all the bath stuff. On to car seats."

He blocked me from pushing the cart away. "This is important," he said, his voice soft but serious.

"I know it is. Did you know you can't bring the baby home from the hospital without it?"

"That's not what I'm talking about."

I forced myself to make eye contact, to be honest. After all, if my parents had been honest with each other, maybe our family wouldn't be splitting apart. "I'm doing my best to get past it."

Connor nodded and buried his hands in his pockets. "It almost feels like it's getting worse. You're always doing stuff for Abbie or with your parents. We don't go out and have fun anymore."

"My family needs me. I can't just blow them off for my boyfriend."

Words eerily similar to the ones Mom had said to me when she wanted me to agree to Hawaii.

"Skylar . . ." Connor's expression made his pain obvious.

I blew my bangs out of my face. Why shouldn't he feel

hurt? I'd basically just told him he wasn't special. "That came out wrong. My family's going through a thing right now. I need to be there." Then quieter, "I don't know how much longer I'll have them."

His fingers curled through mine. "You'll always have me."

He said it with such firmness, such certainty, that I wondered if he was trying to convince himself too.

Mr. Huntley returned our tests at the end of class on Friday the thirteenth. I'd felt okay about my test when I turned it in. I didn't expect an A, but likely a B.

I gaped at my big, ugly score. Sixty-three—a D.

When Connor made grades like this, teachers wrote notes like "What happened?" with a little frowny face. My paper had no frowny face. Teachers expected shoddy work out of me. If I'd made an A, *then* I'd get the "What happened?" note.

Connor called after me as I fled the room. He caught up with me in the hallway. "What's going on? Did you not do well on your test?"

"Sixty-three," I snapped.

"Could you slow down a little?" He huffed as he trotted alongside me. "Sixty-three isn't horrible. There's still lots of time left in the semester."

My teeth clamped into my lower lip. I really didn't want to cry. "Used to be I wouldn't have even cared." That's what really had me irked. I hadn't given 100 percent. I could've studied harder, longer, and that left me dissatisfied. Something I never would've felt before last summer.

I hadn't intended for God to intrude in my schoolwork. Life plans, fine, boundaries with guys, sure, but he couldn't stop there? Apparently he wouldn't be satisfied until he had his finger on every aspect of my life, even a test that couldn't hurt me much. Why couldn't God just accept my half effort? It was more than the other seniors were giving.

"I really don't want to talk about it," I said as I realized Connor continued to rationalize why the test didn't matter.

He shut his mouth.

"Sorry, I didn't mean to snap at you. I'm just frustrated with myself."

"It's fine." He paused. We'd reached the hallway he took to art class, but instead of the usual kiss, he just stood there. "Wanna talk about plans for tomorrow night?"

Right. Valentine's Day.

"Sure."

"I'll come by at seven, okay?"

"Still no clues about what we're doing?"

"If I told you, it wouldn't be a surprise."

I thought of the last surprise, freezing my butt off at the baseball fields. "You do have a knack with surprises."

"I like to think so." Connor ruffled my hair. "See you, girl."

Instead of heading toward English, I watched him saunter down the hall. I wanted everything to be fixed between us, to go back to how it was in the beginning. Before Eli and Jodi got all involved. What did he have planned for tomorrow night? And was I hanging too much hope on it?

"Trouble in paradise?"

I awoke from my thoughts to find Madison standing

there, studying me with those intense eyes of hers. "No. Why?"

"Because you're watching Connor walk away with a frown on your face. Looks like trouble." She leaned toward me, took several exaggerated sniffs, and wrinkled her nose. "Yep. I can smell it."

I laughed. "Stop. You can*not*."

I resumed walking, and she joined me. "So what's the trouble? Did he forget Valentine's Day?"

"No. He's actually got some huge surprise planned."

"That!" Madison stuck her finger in my face. "What's that face?"

"I'm making a face?"

"Totally. You look worried."

"No I don't."

"Yeah you do."

"Well, I'm not worried."

"Well, you look worried."

I rolled my eyes. Clearly we needed a subject change. "What are *your* Valentine's plans?"

"A friend of mine is throwing a big party at her parents' lake house. Girls only. We're gonna burn ex-boyfriend mementos."

"Should be fun."

Madison shrugged her narrow shoulders. "I'm just grateful it falls on a Saturday this year. That means zero chances of seeing Seth sucking face with Ashley."

I grimaced. "Ick. Thanks for the visual."

As we entered English, Madison glanced at Alexis. Something she rarely did. "You and I have spent enough time together over the last few weeks for me to admit this to you." We slid into our seats, and she gave me a sheepish smile. "I always felt a little bit guilty for taking Seth from Alexis. And I was always paranoid that someday the same thing would happen to me."

I'd been at the party last September when Madison caught Seth and Ashley. My friends had laughed at the sight of her sobbing, happy that justice had finally come full circle. I hadn't been one of the laughers, but now I felt slimy inside thinking about how I'd sat there and let it happen.

"Seth's a loser," I said.

"He got too good looking, and it went to his head. Remember back in middle school when he'd follow you, me, and Jodi all over the place? He was so geeky. And not in a cute way."

I smiled. "I'd forgotten about that. Remember when he got in trouble for trying to break into my locker? He was putting flowers or something in there. I can't remember now."

Madison grinned. "Jodi was so mad about that."

"She was?" I glanced at my former friend, who picked at her cuticles while jabbering with Alexis. "Over *Seth*?"

"Of course. You know, Jodi was the queen before you started school there. You dethroned her, and not just with cool guys but with losers like Seth."

"It's a wonder we were ever friends."

She tipped her head toward me. "Or maybe you never really were."

On paper, it all looked good.
A dozen roses—check.
Jewelry—check.

A sweet, sappy card—check.

A nice restaurant—check, check, check.

That's right, three restaurants.

We picked up carryout from P.F. Chang's—lettuce wraps with that to-die-for ginger plum sauce. We sat at Mill Creek Park on the edge of one of the fountains and watched other dates go on around us. Then we walked to McCormick and Schmick's for crazy-good seafood. When he said I couldn't order dessert, I pouted until we landed at the Cheesecake Factory. Chocolate peanut butter cookie dough cheesecake. Enough said.

And as if all that walking around hadn't been enough, we topped this off with a nice stroll around the Plaza.

"You really like it?" Connor asked me for the thousandth time.

I caressed the wide, silver bracelet he'd given me to start off the night. "I do. I love it."

"Really?"

"Really."

He still looked cautious. "You're intimidating to pick out jewelry for. I finally went with the one Cameron liked the best."

"Well, Cameron has impeccable taste." I turned my bracelet in the light of the streetlamp. "The way he wears the shirt from his train pajamas with the pants of his Superman pajamas? Talk about fashion forward."

Connor tucked his arm around me and surveyed the bustling shopping district. "So what do you think? A good surprise?"

"It was too much," I said. "The flowers, all the restaurants . . . You really didn't have to do that."

"But I wanted to." He touched his nose to mine and nuzzled. "You should be treated special."

And yet I'd felt much more special the night we ate cold subs while shivering on a deserted baseball field. It had been sweet, personal, and we'd been so comfortable with each other. There hadn't been land mines to step around, not like now. Tonight, though lavish and romantic, seemed generic. And—I couldn't seem to shake this thought—desperate.

"What are you thinking about?" Connor asked. "Let me guess." He tapped his chin, feigning deep thought. "You're thinking, Man, I wish he'd just shut up and kiss me."

I forced a smile. "That's it."

And as he leaned close to me, I wondered if my mom was right. Maybe sometimes it wasn't worth it to stick around and fix things. Maybe sometimes you should just cut your losses and move on.

19

Store window displays moved on to St. Patty's themes, but at school, St. Valentine still ruled the halls in anticipation of the Sweetheart dance.

Abbie had never been much for school functions, but now with Chris in the picture, she looked forward to the dance like Christmas morning. We hit most maternity stores in the metro area in our quest for the perfect dress. While I chased away any saleslady who dared to be snotty with my sister, Abbie tried on formal after formal until we finally had success.

So not until Saturday morning—the day of the dance—did I realize *I* didn't have a dress.

Or not a new dress anyway. It seemed in poor taste to recycle a dress I'd worn to a dance with another guy, particularly Eli. Strange—I'd looked forward to buying or making something special for my first dance with Connor. Yet another thing to have gotten lost in the shuffle.

"Can't you just wear one of mine?" Abbie asked when I explained why I was throwing my hair up in a ponytail and rushing out the door without showering.

I paused. Before the baby, we'd been about the same size, give or take an inch. Why not?

Abbie left for her mani-pedi and granted me freedom to peruse her closet.

As I leafed through Abbie's clothes—cute and designer branded, but too generic for my taste—my heart pounded as I imagined the possibilities. New buttons for that sweater. A cropped hemline for that blazer—maybe a new, bold lining. And that polo . . . I pulled it out for closer inspection. Okay, I couldn't do anything to rescue this one from its boring life, but everything else . . .

No. I pushed aside the clothes and focused on the formals shoved to the back. Now that I'd committed to nursing, I needed to give up all those useless hours I'd put into clothes. Shopping, sewing, fantasizing. I'd use my sewing machine only for useful projects, like the bedding for Abbie's baby, or . . . Well, surely I'd come up with other things.

I whipped a classic black dress from the back of the closet, calf-length with a gathered skirt that would look great when Connor twirled me across the dance floor. Though to spice it up, I could make a red—

No.

No, no, no.

I marched myself out of Abbie's room and into the bathroom, determined to use my shower to scrub away my fashion obsession.

Abbie looked stunning.

Not despite being pregnant—she was just plain gorgeous. She wore her hair in big, loose curls, her smile sparkled, and the dress we'd found—a shimmery eggplant—did something to bring out her cinnamon eyes.

Abbie twirled before us, a look of uncertainty creasing her forehead. "What do you guys think?"

"Gorgeous," I said. "I can't wait to see Chris's face."

"Really?" Abbie smoothed her dress around her tummy for possibly the thousandth time.

"Really. You look great." I appealed to Mom and Dad, who, strangely, both sat in the living room. Dad fussed with bills, and Mom hadn't taken her gaze off the TV since we walked in. "Doesn't she look great?"

Dad looked up and smiled. "You both look very beautiful."

"Mom?" I prompted.

"Very nice." Her voice sounded as frosty as the weather. Apparently she'd yet to recover from the idea of Abbie going to the dance. Why would Abbie choose to live with her? She couldn't even seem to understand that this was Abbie's last high school hurrah.

The doorbell rang, and Abbie and I rushed to answer it. I expected only Connor and Chris but opened the door to find the entire Ross family, Cevin included.

Amy leaned close for a hug. "I hope you don't mind our intrusion. I told the boys I couldn't miss the photo op."

My mind raced to the chilly scene Abbie and I had just left—Mom and Dad sitting like two sulking children in the living room. "Sure, come in." I tried to infuse my voice with warmth. They wouldn't find it anywhere else in this house.

Amy gasped at my sister. "Abigail Marie, don't you look beautiful! Turn around for me. Oh, that dress is perfect."

Would that have been so hard for Mom to do?

Abbie beamed at the praise. "Skylar helped me."

"I can tell." Amy touched the funky beads I'd draped around my sister's neck last minute.

Okay, so I knew I wasn't supposed to be doing the fashion thing anymore, but I couldn't help it when I saw Abbie's bare neck. She could help wean me. Like how smokers have nicotine patches.

Although, the way Abbie beamed—so confident of being beautiful and loved—I was tempted to raid her closet and start all the other improvement projects I'd thought of.

Connor took one of my hands. "Hey, beautiful."

My smile froze on my face as I spotted the corsage—two enormous flowers adorned with thick, long ribbons like streamers. Good thing I'd decided there were more important things than looking good.

He started to push it over my hand when Amy stopped him.

"I can't get a good picture in this light. Where's the switch?"

"Why not come into the living room?" Mom asked. Apparently at some point, she and Dad had joined us.

I watched for Amy's reaction to my mom. They hadn't seen each other since Mom had returned. Amy smiled, still warm, but a little tight. "Hi, Teri. Sorry for invading your home."

"Not at all. We should have thought to invite you over." Mom glanced at Cevin, who wriggled in Curtis's arms, desperate to get down and explore.

Brian must have noticed Mom's less-than-welcoming gaze. He took Cevin from his son's skinny arms. "I'll hold him while we're inside, buddy. We don't want him getting loose in the Hoyts' house and getting hair everywhere."

As I followed the parade into the living room, I burned with shame at my mother's frigid behavior. I'd never met anybody nicer than the Rosses. They'd always opened their home to Abbie and me, always made themselves available. I didn't like seeing them treated so coldly.

Connor's fingertips brushed the back of my neck. "I can't believe how lucky I am. You look amazing."

I blushed. He looked good too, especially when he smiled at me like that. Made it easy to forgive the T. rex corsage.

After a few awkward pictures—no one seemed quite sure how to position Chris and Abbie—we headed out for dinner. At Sonic Drive-In.

Seriously.

Abbie had a hankering for corn dogs and convinced the guys to cancel the reservation at the Italian place.

"I'm agreeing to this on one condition only," Connor said as he steered his SUV into a slot. "If anybody asks, Chris and I fully planned on taking you girls out for a nice dinner."

Abbie leaned forward for a better look at the menu. "Ooh, chili cheese Coney. I haven't had one of those in forever."

"What happened to corn dogs?" I asked.

"They don't come with chili and cheese."

"Stop leaning over me." I nudged her backward. "I don't want you drooling all over my jacket."

She giggled and pantomimed licking my coat.

"Ew, gross." I swatted her away.

Connor's fingers cupped my knee. "What are you hungry for?"

In the backseat, Abbie giggled about something with

Chris. She sure seemed in a good mood for someone on the verge of teen motherhood. Chris's spirits, I noticed, were muted. Even for him.

Connor placed our order, then we chatted as we waited. Or three of us did. Chris really did seem out of sorts. When he caught me watching him, he smiled a strange, tight smile and looked away.

Abbie bounced in her seat. "Food's here!"

Connor rolled down his window and said hi to the tiny brunette carhop.

"Hey." She handed him the bags of food and grinned at our formal wear. "Too late to make reservations?"

Connor sighed as Abbie and I giggled. "Don't get me started." When the carhop left, Connor gave me a pained expression. "I bet she thinks I'm some horrible, cheap boy-friend."

I unwrapped my BLT. "Should we ring her back so I can tell her you took me to three restaurants on Valentine's Day?"

"Can we please?" he said with a wink.

If only I knew of a way to tell him this was way better—and somehow more romantic—than our dinner tour on the Plaza.

"Oh my gosh, this is so good," Abbie said through an enormous bite of Coney. "Skylar, remember Dad's friend who owns those Sonics? With that creepy son who followed you around that one summer?"

"Yeah."

"Dump Connor and marry him."

Abbie and I both dissolved into giggles. When did I last have fun? Just let go and laugh so long my stomach ached? This night would be fantastic.

"Do they have Sonic in Hawaii?" Chris asked.

We all stared at him, and I felt my carefree night draining away.

"I don't know," Abbie said in a careful voice. She didn't look at him. "I doubt it."

"I'm sure somebody on the islands makes Coneys." Connor held out his fries to me. "Have one. They're perfect."

"Have you and your mom found a place yet?" Chris peered innocently at Abbie while sucking on his straw.

"Not yet."

"What kind of place are you looking for?"

"I don't know. Mom's taking care of it." Her appetite must have slowed. Now she just stared at her dinner.

I gave Connor what I hoped was a "do something" look.

"Who likes my tie?" he asked, raising his own hand. "Two dollars."

Abbie, Chris, and I all blinked at him. He couldn't come up with anything better?

"Have you set a moving date yet?" Chris asked.

Abbie stabbed at her hot dog. "You know, I'm not moving tonight, or even in the next month, so why don't we just drop the subject and enjoy ourselves?"

"Sure." Chris popped a cheesy tater tot into his mouth. "We wouldn't want to talk about anything serious, would we? That might spoil our *fun*." He said *fun* like it tasted bad.

Abbie glared at him. "What does that mean?"

"Chris, now probably isn't—" But Connor had intervened too late.

"You're so busy having fun, you don't realize you're hurting other people," Chris said, his volume escalating with each word. Since when did he talk so much?

"In case you haven't noticed, my fun has an expiration date on it." Abbie jabbed her stomach with her thumb. "So, sorry I don't want to sit around and mope about the baby and Hawaii with you. I'd rather enjoy our last dance together."

"It's not just me. It's your sister."

"Me?" I said.

Abbie looked from Chris to me, then back to Chris. "What?"

"You're so busy avoiding the baby, Skylar's having to pick up your slack."

Abbie laughed one of her big, dramatic laughs. "Avoiding the baby? I *can't* avoid the baby. You think I just popped into Macy's and grabbed this dress? You think I sleep well at night with her using my bladder as a trampoline? I *know* I'm having a baby, Chris."

"What are you naming her?" Chris's question seemed quiet and gentle compared to Abbie's yelling.

Her face clouded over. "I haven't decided. You know that."

"What are some options? Some thoughts you've had?"

"I'm not . . . I don't . . ."

"You're not what? You don't what?"

Connor leaned toward me. "Why don't we give them some privacy?"

"You guys don't need to leave." Chris's tone pinned me to my seat. "You certainly fight in front of us plenty."

I glanced at Abbie. She looked at me, pleading for a rescue. "Chris, why don't we hold off on this conversation? Maybe have it after the dance."

Chris ignored this advice. "I know you're scared, Abbie, and I get it. But you have to pick a name. You have to buy diapers. You have to make plans. You can't just leave everything up to your mom and Skylar." He reached for her hand, clasped it between his own. "And you can't go to Hawaii."

Abbie, whose head had been ducked with shame, looked up at him. "What?"

"You can't go to Hawaii."

"I . . ." Abbie swallowed. "I have to go."

"No you don't."

"But my mom—"

"Your mom will be fine."

"But Lance and everyone here—"

"That's why you want to go?" Chris said. "To get away from Lance and anyone who might disapprove?"

"I guess." Abbie fussed with her necklace. "It just sounds good, you know? Getting away."

"Leaving won't solve anything," I said. How hypocritical. As if I hadn't been fantasizing about running off to Hawaii as well.

"Mom'll be really mad if I back out." Abbie offered Chris a sweet smile, her eyelashes fluttering, and adjusted his boutonniere with her free hand.

I knew then Abbie would stay.

❀

"How cute are they?"

Connor followed my gaze to the gymnasium bleachers, where Chris and Abbie sat. She had her legs tossed onto his lap, and he smiled at her like she was a prize of some sort. It made me want to squeeze him with gratefulness.

"Looks like things will work out well for them."

I beamed and rewarded his words with a kiss. "And for us."

Connor spun me away from him, then yanked me back close. This appeared to be his signature dance move. He'd already done it about four times and seemed to thrive on surprising me. "You did much better that time. No stumbling."

"I'd like to see you stay on your feet in three-inch heels."

His nose wrinkled. "No thank you."

I smiled as he drew me against him.

The dance had been going for about an hour. Lance brought that trampy gossip Marie Green, but Abbie hadn't seemed to notice. I'd seen Madison dancing happily enough with a guy she'd invited from her work. As for the Lisa-John-Alexis triangle, Lisa had danced at least once with John, but I'd also seen her chatting up one of the German foreign exchange students.

"Uh-oh. Incoming," Connor muttered into my ear.

I barely had time to say, "What?" when I felt a tap on my shoulder and turned to see Eli standing there.

"Hey, guys. How's it going?" He grinned at me, his white teeth gleaming. "We're starting the after party a little early out at John's. You two wanna come?"

"No thanks." Connor gripped me tighter. Or maybe his fingers just adjusted, I couldn't be sure.

"Suit yourselves." Eli winked at me. "Lookin' good, Skylar."

He swaggered away, maybe already a little drunk.

Connor rolled his eyes. "What's wrong with him? Saying that kind of stuff right in front of me?"

Unlike Jodi, who had the class to say it when I was gone?

But I bit the words back. Tonight things had felt normal between us, and it was oh so nice.

"At least they're all leaving." I nodded toward the door where Eli helped Jodi into her coat. She laughed at something he said.

"She's going with them?" Connor groaned. "I thought she'd given all that up."

I didn't know what to say. I felt a little proud to be proven right, though I wished I didn't.

As if sensing this, Connor smiled at me, gentle and appreciative. "I guess you're not surprised."

"But maybe you planted some seeds with her." I snuggled closer. "Her going out tonight doesn't mean it's all lost."

"Yeah, maybe." He continued to look doubtful.

I grabbed his hand and spun him away from me, then pulled him back in. Connor stumbled, and we knocked into another couple, both of us laughing so hard we could barely apologize.

"Nice move, Hoyt." He matched his forehead to mine, and when he looked in my eyes, I knew Hawaii couldn't offer a thing that came close to this.

20

"Skylar, the baby's coming."

I jolted out of sleep to find Abbie perched on the edge of my bed, one hand clutching her belly. In her braided pigtails and cartoon pj's, she looked even more like a kid.

Her voice wobbled as she said, "I'm having contractions."

"Have you been timing them? The book says they should be four minutes apart." I thanked God that I'd read that part the day before.

"I want to go to the hospital."

I looked at the clock—2:42. I'd been asleep for maybe an hour. My brain had been too abuzz with thoughts of the dance for me to doze off.

I flipped on my bedside lamp. "Where's the pregnancy book?"

"I don't know." Abbie shielded her eyes. "Who cares about the book? Let's just go."

I spotted it on my desk and threw back the covers. "Take deep breaths or lie down or something."

"I want to go to the hospital."

"I know," I said, maybe a little sharper than necessary. "But lie down, okay? I want to see what else the book says. We don't want to go to the hospital if we don't need to."

"We need to. The baby's coming." But she curled up under my blankets. "Skylar, I don't have a name."

"You'll come up with one."

"We don't have a crib. Or diapers. Or clothes."

"Yes we do."

"We do?"

"In the guest bedroom. Everything's still in the packaging, but it's in there."

"You did that for me?" Abbie asked through a yawn.

"Quiet, I'm trying to read." I scanned the page. "Okay, you're supposed to have contractions every four minutes, lasting for a minute or longer, for one hour. Then we go to the hospital."

"When does my water break?"

"It doesn't say."

Another yawn. "Did you buy a car seat? We have to have one to bring her home."

"The safest one they make."

"Okay, good." Long pause. I thought she'd dozed off, but then she said, "She needs a name."

"She'll have one. Just relax."

"I want to go to the hospital."

By now I'd stopped looking through the book. I just sat there watching her. Sure enough, within a couple minutes, Abbie's breathing deepened as she dozed off.

I tugged on slippers and relocated to the living room. Unlike my last three a.m. trek downstairs, I found the place dark and isolated. Using the moonlight and my memory, I groped my way to the couch and collapsed. My heart still thundered from Abbie's words—*"The baby's coming."*

What a terrifying sentence.

I didn't know how to change a diaper, calm a fussy baby, give a bath, use the car seat . . . and the list went on and on. Yet why should I be scared? She wasn't my baby. Abbie would be doing all those things.

I remembered standing in Babies R Us, overwhelmed by the choices of cribs and car seats and strollers. Where'd Abbie been while I agonized over these decisions? Seeing a movie with her friends? Parked in front of the TV? Doing anything and everything to avoid thinking that she had no idea what her life looked like after March 10?

A new thought chilled me—what did *my* life look like after March 10?

I'd offered to help, but we'd never defined what that meant. Running to the store for diapers? Watching her while Abbie went to school? Midnight feedings?

My head throbbed with the possibilities of what this baby meant for me. It wasn't fair. I'd been good. I'd abstained. Why should I have to deal with Abbie's consequences? All I wanted to do this summer was lounge by the pool with Connor. Maybe eat some ice cream. But could I ever feel good about leaving the house, about continuing with my life, while the baby had Abbie chained at home? With Mom in Hawaii and Dad working, she'd really only have me.

I buried my face in the scratchy throw pillow. It was too late—or too early—for these kinds of thoughts. I should think about Connor instead, about the way he'd looked at me, the way he'd kissed me good night. With that happy thought, I snuggled into the couch as best I could and fell asleep.

The black-and-white bathing suit.

I'm in a house, a little house. It's Grammy and Papa's, but they're nowhere around. It's just me here in the paneled living room. The doors and windows are all open, allowing in the salty breeze, the sounds of rustling foliage. I want to go outside but can't move. That stuff I bought at Babies R Us for Abbie—the bathtub, the cloth diapers, everything—is scattered at my feet. But Abbie and the baby aren't here. They're back in Kansas. Nothing around me says it, it's just one of those things I know.

Mom walks into the room and surveys all the baby junk. "Look at this mess you made, Skylar. Clean this up."

I look around. "I don't know where to start."

She opens her mouth and says . . .

"Something wrong with your bed upstairs?"

I cracked open my eyelids to find Mom standing in front of the couch. She appeared to have slept much better than me. Her dark hair was pulled back in a loose but mess-free ponytail, and her expensive cotton jammies were wrinkle-free.

"Abbie's in it." I stretched. "She freaked out that the baby was coming, said she was having contractions, but then she fell asleep."

"Mmm, Braxton Hicks." Mom sipped at her coffee. "I had those all the time with you."

"What are they?"

"Braxton Hicks contractions. They're like mini contractions getting your body ready for labor." Mom took a seat in the wingback chair. "Hard to believe there's going to be a baby around."

I sat up and finger-combed my hair into the best ponytail I could. I always felt uncomfortable around Mom if I hadn't groomed myself.

She looked at me with big, round eyes. "I so wish you'd come to Kapaa with us, Sky-baby."

Tears blinded me. Mom hadn't called me that for years. It reminded me of the little house, back when Mom giggled with Abbie and me and seemed to delight in us. Could it ever be like that again, or was it time to cut my losses with Mom?

"I don't know," I whispered.

Her face brightened ever so slightly. "Have you been thinking about it?"

I nodded. "I have these dreams . . ."

But did the dreams mean I was supposed to be in Hawaii or that it would be a disaster? Or did they mean anything at all? Were they just a result of me dwelling on Hawaii?

"I think it'd be good for you to get away from all this." Mom fluttered her hand, as if to indicate this house, this life. As if it wasn't something she'd helped create. "Try it just for the summer. You can always come back."

I wound the drawstring of my pants around my finger, then unwound it. I thought of last night at the dance, Connor spinning me away and pulling me close. "I might come for a week or two, but no more than that. Connor . . ."

I couldn't finish. I knew Mom would think me stupid for imagining myself in love at this age. Maybe I was stupid, though I couldn't shake this feeling that ultimately Connor was who I'd be with. But marriage was a long way off. What about the in-between time?

"Connor is nobody to base your life plans on," Mom said. "I know you care about him a great deal, but don't let him hold you back. Don't give up anything for him."

Could I trust Mom, or did she speak from that angry place inside of her, the place that said she'd given up her life for my father and he'd cheated on her?

I'd spent enough time at the Ross house to see everything Amy gave up. Surely she'd rather do stuff besides cook and fold laundry, but she did it for Brian, for her kids. She saw it as a worthy sacrifice. But would she still think so if Brian up and left her?

If it weren't for Connor, I'd have hopped at the chance to go to Hawaii. If I truly loved him, like I knew I did, was the experience an acceptable thing to give up? I didn't know.

"Let's just say I'm still thinking about it," I said to Mom in a crisp, end-of-discussion kind of voice.

She tuned the TV in to a political show. I went upstairs to boot Abbie out of my room and get dressed for church.

21

"I have to tell you something." Lisa had a skittish look about her, like a puppy who'd peed on the rug.

I sighed and closed my locker door. "Did you get back together with John?"

She looked me in the eye. "No! I told you it was over with him."

"You've said that before."

Her brow wrinkled. "I'm changing. I told you."

"Who isn't these days?" I said, then grimaced. It wasn't that I didn't want Lisa to change. Or Jodi. I just didn't want her grabbing onto my boyfriend in the process.

"That's kinda what I need to talk to you about." Lisa glanced around the emptying hallway. The bell could ring any second, but I had study hall and didn't care. Whatever class Lisa had next, she didn't seem in any hurry to get there. Or to get to her point.

I hitched my bag up on my shoulder. "Where are you headed? I'll walk with you."

"I think it'd be best to do this somewhere hidden," Lisa said. "Certain people might see."

I raised my eyebrows. "Certain people whose names begin with J and A? Why do you care what they think?"

Lisa's jaw clenched. "You know, maybe I don't have anything to say after all. Maybe I just imagined Jodi leaving the party Saturday night with Connor."

"What do you mean?"

My mind ticked through Saturday night's events. We'd stayed until the end of the dance—a first for Abbie and me. Connor and Chris took us home. Abbie fell asleep in the car. Connor kissed me good night. I lugged Abbie upstairs. I looked at the clock as I fell into bed—12:14.

Lisa gave me a wary look. "Will you stop being a snot?"

I swallowed the nasty response waiting on the end of my tongue. "Yes."

"Here's what I know." Lisa dropped her voice, as if the lockers might be bugged. "Jodi was wasted. I mean, toilet-hugging drunk. She made a phone call, and ten minutes later I saw Connor helping her out of the party. They sat in his car for, like, fifteen minutes, and then he drove off."

She evaluated me, as if expecting a barrage of questions. I could barely process this information, much less think of a response.

"I don't know who all saw," Lisa continued. "I know Eli didn't. He was upstairs with some trampy girl when Jodi called Connor."

"I don't think it means anything." I tried to sound sure of this. To not think about yesterday at church. Or our phone conversation yesterday afternoon. Or this morning when he brought Abbie and me to school. All those opportunities to tell me.

Lisa shrugged. "Maybe not." But I could tell she doubted.

"I'm sure he was just giving her a ride home. She probably didn't have anyone else to call."

"I'm sure that's all it was."

But those fifteen minutes that she'd seen them sitting in the car . . .

"And how much had you been drinking? Maybe it seemed like they sat out there for a long time, but they really didn't."

"I only had a beer or two. And I'm pretty sure I looked at the clock. But . . ." She shrugged again. "Maybe it really was just a couple minutes."

"Or maybe it *was* longer, but it's because Jodi threw up or something."

"Certainly wouldn't be the first time."

"And maybe—"

"Maybe there's someone else you should be talking to." Lisa gave me a pointed look. "*He* will actually have answers."

I forced myself to think about Connor, about what his answers might be. Giving Jodi a ride home, I could rationalize. Him not telling me, I couldn't. That meant something, didn't it?

"You're right," I said to Lisa. I took a couple steps back, toward Connor's English class. "Thanks for telling me."

"Good luck," she called after me.

Halfway to Connor's class, the tears came and couldn't be stopped. I ducked into a bathroom, grateful to find it vacant. As I bawled on the dingy bathroom floor, I tallied my losses.

Since putting my life back in God's hands, Abbie had gotten pregnant, my parents' marriage teetered on the edge of failure, I'd lost all my friends and my first boyfriend, and I was about to lose my second.

Maybe it wasn't right to blame God. Maybe it would've happened anyway, and he was the only reason for my survival.

"Do you have answers?" I asked. "Can you fix this? Hawaii, Connor, my ready-to-pop sister?"

Like my dad, I'd never been good at praying. I had a rough time converting my thoughts into words. The same trouble I had with people. But luckily, unlike people, God was bigger than my loss for words.

I squeezed my eyes shut. "Because I don't know what to do. I just don't know."

I once thought I'd had it all figured out. But now I knew I didn't. With a certainty I'd never before felt, I knew I was clueless. Should I stay with Connor? Was this a losing battle with him and Jodi? Should my parents stay together? Should I go to Hawaii? I didn't know any of it.

"I just want whatever's best," I whispered. "I just want you to take all these decisions and make them for me."

He didn't seem to be answering. Should I be able to hear him? Did it mean I'd prayed wrong if I didn't feel peaceful or have clear direction?

I heard voices approaching the bathroom and scurried off the floor.

I didn't make eye contact with either of the entering girls, couldn't have described anything about them other than their poor taste in shoes.

But they knew me.

"Can you believe the administration's still letting her sister come to school?" one said to the other as the door swung closed. "She's so pregnant, it's gross."

"I bet her dad paid them off," the second girl said.

Their words burned, as did the surge of fresh tears. The old me would've marched back into that bathroom and given those girls a piece of my mind. The old me would've defended Abbie, even if we weren't that close.

For the first time, I liked the old Skylar much better. The new one just hung her head and slunk away.

Just how long did Connor plan on waiting before telling me about Jodi? Surely he knew it couldn't be kept a secret. Even if he and Jodi swore to take it to the grave, wouldn't he suspect someone might have seen him hauling her drunk butt out of John's house?

And even if he knew beyond a doubt there was no way I'd find out, this was still Connor we were talking about. Connor who didn't believe in dishonesty. Connor who prided himself on getting all the cards out on the table. On being the same in the dark as in the light.

I decided I'd like to know just how long it would take him to fess up. I wouldn't say a word of what Lisa told me. And if someone brought up the party, I might go so far as to pretend I'd forgotten it happened in the first place. Then, when Connor finally did tell me, I'd make him feel really guilty.

The plan seemed genius. Until I saw him.

He smiled when he saw me coming out of study hall. "Hey, good lookin'. Going my way?"

I cringed when he put his arm around me.

"I think we should go out tonight," Connor said as we headed toward our horribly boring Health Sciences class. "It's been forever since the two of us went out."

"You mean besides Sweetheart on Saturday?" My voice had a rasp to it, like it often got if I'd cried a lot. Connor didn't seem to notice.

"That doesn't count. We were with Chris and Abbie."

"Well, I can't." I crossed my arms over my chest. "I promised Abbie we'd hang out tonight."

Connor frowned. "You can't hang out some other night?"

"We need to get the baby's room ready."

His frown deepened. "Can't you do that tomorrow night?"

I shook my head. "Abbie wants to get it done before this weekend."

"What's this weekend?"

"The winter retreat. Remember?"

"Right." He scratched the back of his head. "Well, I guess we'll spend time together there. Nothing says romance like the entire youth group in rural Missouri."

"Like you care about romance."

Connor feigned outrage. "Excuse me, but I'm always romantic. You're the one without a romantic bone in her body."

"That's not true."

"It is. Especially recently. I'm always the one remembering our anniversary, coming up with Valentine's arrangements—"

I yanked away from him. "That's enough. I've got a lot going on, okay? I'm struggling to make decent grades for the first time in my life. My sister's about to have a baby. My mom keeps pushing me about coming to Hawaii with her. Does it sound like I have time for anything else right now?"

He glanced at the other students streaming around us, then took my hands and squeezed them. "I don't mean to be hard on you, Skylar. It's just . . ." He shook his head. "Recently I feel like your attention is always divided. You're thinking about Abbie or your parents. And I know those are big things going on in your life, but I just wish you'd open up to me more about them."

"Sure, open up more." Despite my fury, my voice sounded eerily calm. "That's really the problem here. Me."

Connor blinked at this. "You're mad."

"Yes, I am."

"Why?"

"Why? Tell me why you think I'd be mad."

Connor sighed and raked his hands through his hair. "Come on, Skylar. You know I hate that kind of stuff. Let's just get it all out on the table."

"Yeah. Go ahead. Get it out on the table." I took a step back and gave him an icy glare with only minimal effort. "You have plenty to share, don't you? From Saturday night?"

Connor's face froze in horror. "*That's* what this is about."

"Yeah." I pulled my arms tight against my chest, like I could protect myself. "Lisa told me."

"Look, I know I should've told you, but it wasn't a big deal—"

I rolled my eyes. "Oh, spare me, Connor," I said as I marched away.

He jogged to catch up. "She needed a ride home, I took her home. That was it. I didn't tell you because I knew you'd freak out."

"No. I'm freaking out *because* you didn't tell me."

"You'd have freaked out either way and you know it."

"No." We'd reached a quieter part of the hallway, so I pulled to the side and stopped walking. "This doesn't get to be about what's wrong with me, okay? It's not about my insecurities or all the ways I might have screwed up. This is about you not telling me something you *know* you should have."

He swallowed and nodded slowly. "You're right. I should've told you."

"I told you she was the end of us."

"I know you did. I'm sorry."

"What's the deal with her?" I forced myself to ask. I hoped I wouldn't cry again. "Why can't you just leave her alone?"

"Skylar, she needs someone stable in her life. That's all I'm trying to be."

And that's when it dawned on me. "I get it now." So Connor had flaws after all. "It's not *just* about being there for her, is it?"

"Of course that's all it is," he said crossly. "I've been telling you that the whole time."

"No. It's about *fixing* her. Just like you fixed me."

"It's not like that," Connor said, each syllable measured and heavy.

I'd seen him angry like this only once before—my eighteenth birthday when I'd suggested he wanted to be my boyfriend, but Connor hadn't been ready to admit it to himself. It would only be a matter of time before he realized I was right about this too.

"It is. And I can't be in a relationship like this. We have

no chance of being happy and normal because you need to be swooping in and saving the day."

"I'm not listening to another word of this lunacy," Connor said before stalking away.

And that's how we ended. Him walking away and me standing there, reeling from what had just happened.

I'd lost him.

22

"You're sure you don't mind me going?"

"I have more than enough to do." Abbie looked up from assembling a bouncy seat. "I have a kid to name, a room to decorate, a bag to pack . . ."

"Our bag is packed." I raised my bed skirt, revealing the red duffle bag.

Abbie sighed. "No wonder Chris yelled at me. You've taken care of everything. Even bedding."

Her smile transformed into a grimace, and she clutched her stomach with both hands. I knew by then not to say anything, just to watch the clock and wait. After twentyish seconds, she released her stomach and resumed normal breathing.

"How many today?" I asked.

"That's the first one."

All week this had gone on, starting with the night of the Sweetheart dance. Contractions started, happened off and on for thirty minutes, and then faded away. The doctor said this was normal, and it would still likely be weeks until the baby came. Considering the disheveled state of the nursery, weeks still felt too soon.

I turned to my closet and reached for a group of shirts. "Any luck on names?"

"If it was a boy, I'd be done."

"Well, it's a girl."

"I know." Abbie sighed and rubbed her belly. "It's really hard. I mean, this will be her name *forever*. For better or worse. Think about it."

"I'm sure you'll pick a great one."

"I might just have to see her first." Abbie gaped. "What are those?"

I blushed and shoved them deep into my duffle bag. "Nothing. Just some shirts I picked up."

Abbie snorted. "They're plain tees. Since when do you buy plain tees?"

"I just liked them, okay?" I caught myself tugging at my hair and stuffed my hands in my pockets. I wished she'd stop with the critical looks.

"Since when do you like anything plain?" She pointed at me. "And that shirt you're wearing. I saw that for seven dollars at J.Crew! What's with you?"

I crossed my arms over my chest, as if it could hide my striped top. "I just thought it was time for a new look."

"A boring look?"

"Not boring. Classic. Simple."

"Boring."

"Stop saying *boring*," I huffed, turning back to my packing.

I'd never bought anything on clearance. When things were priced to move—and at $6.99 a pop, these shirts definitely were—it meant they moved right into the closet of everyone who saw them. And that's when you showed up at a party wearing the same thing as every other girl.

But with Connor out of my life, basically no friends, and

a strange slowdown in schoolwork, I'd found myself with an excess of free time. So I'd indulged in a little retail therapy. I usually avoided the back of stores so I wouldn't even be tempted by the good deals, but I wasn't in my usual shopping spirits. My heart didn't feel like being at the mall. It felt like returning to bed and having a good long cry. And in my distracted state, I wandered too far in. Before I could stop myself and get out of there, I spotted the shirts—so soft and comfy and discounted.

I rationalized the purchase with the knowledge that I'd been accepted to Johnson County's nursing program. Having officially turned away from textiles, it was pointless to devote so much energy and money to clothing. These shirts—cotton long-sleeve tees in varying earth tones—would still be in style years from now. I could stop my endless cycle of buying new clothes every season. Maybe I'd even go a whole year without buying something new . . .

"Skylar, you okay? You look kinda panicked."

"I'm fine. Honestly." I pushed the shirts deeper into the bag and covered them with a couple pairs of jeans. My new boring—no, classic—style made packing a breeze.

"Sneakers?" Abbie said as I tied my shoes. "Okay, what's going on with you? I haven't seen you wear sneakers in forever."

"It's a youth retreat. I don't exactly need my Manolos."

She shrugged. "If you say so. But you're just not Skylar without your weirdly amazing clothes."

It reminded me of a time not long ago, when Connor asked if I thought dressing unique made me unique. I'd feared it for a while now, that I'd let my clothes become so big a part of my identity that I couldn't be separated from them.

"I half thought you'd cancel," Connor said, throwing my bag into the back of Amy's van. Brian had signed up to chaperone. "I didn't think Abbie'd want you leaving."

"The doctor said lots of women start having contractions a few weeks out." I shrugged. "I guess it's a longer process than they show on TV. Did you know most of the time the water doesn't even break? They have to break it for you."

"Gross."

I sat on the curb and crossed my legs at the ankles. Around us, parents dropped off students while youth coaches shoved bags into vehicles. I missed Heather. She'd make all this bearable. Just a few more days until she returned from Uganda.

Connor took a seat next to me, careful to put distance between us. We hadn't talked much since our fight on Monday, just necessary exchanges like, "Hello," and, "Can I turn down the radio, or are you listening to this?"

I hadn't told anybody about our breakup. It looked like he'd been putting it off too.

"So. This is awkward," Connor said. "I don't think we've been alone since that really great chat on Monday."

I gestured to the parking lot full of activity. "We're not alone."

"You know what I mean."

I shrugged. I should've backed out of this thing, especially since I knew Jodi planned to come and things were bound to get even more awkward than this.

203

"I really am sorry," Connor said. "About all of it. Giving her a ride home. You having to hear about it from Lisa."

I shrugged again. "It doesn't matter."

And it didn't. Not now, anyway. It had happened and we'd broken up. If we hadn't broken up Monday, it would've happened eventually. Now we should both focus on moving on.

I felt Connor evaluate my outfit.

"You know, you've been dressing differently the last few days." He cocked his head and studied my shirt, jeans, and sneakers. "No animal prints. No funky jewelry. I kinda miss it."

"I so don't want to talk about it." I rested my palms on the cold, hard ground and leaned back.

Connor frowned. "Is something going on?"

"It's none of your business."

His frown deepened. "If something's going on with you, I'd like to think you'd tell me about it."

"Why?" I scoffed. "Because we used to date?"

His eyes widened at this. "*Used* to?"

I turned away. "We broke up on Monday." How could he not know this?

"No we didn't."

"I told you Jodi was the end of us, and you basically told me you felt you had to be 'stable' for her."

"You're inferring a breakup from that?" He pulled his hands through his hair, making it stick out in all directions. He needed to get it cut. "That was just a fight, Skylar."

"No, it was a breakup."

"It was a fight."

"Okay, fine. Then *this* is a breakup. We're broken up."

"Stop being hurt and stubborn for, like, two seconds and really think about this, okay?" When I wouldn't look at him, he moved in front of my face. "I love *you*. I want to be with *you*. Do you believe that?"

My insides warmed with his words. Only God could provide the strength for me to get through this. "It's not that I doubt any of that, Connor, and I'm not saying it's over forever. I'm saying you have something you need to work out. Until you resolve your need to fix every broken girl you come across, I don't think we should be together."

Eli ambled over to us. "Hey, guys. What's going on?"

"Can you give us a minute?" Connor practically barked at him. "We're in the middle of something."

Eli splayed his hands, surrendering, and backed away.

"You could've asked him a little nicer," I said.

"He's a big boy. He can deal with it." Connor claimed my fingers, and I fought away thoughts of how much I'd miss him. "Please don't break up with me."

"Please stop asking me that," I whispered.

Connor watched my twitching left eye. "Skylar, you have every right to be mad at me. I get it. But this is nothing we can't work through."

I took a wobbly breath. "When you work through it— when you're no longer in love with the idea of rescuing Jodi—then we'll talk."

I pried my fingers from his and joined Eli, who loitered by one of the vans, looking unsure.

He grinned when he spotted me coming his way. "Everything cool?"

I shrugged. "Yeah." Luckily Eli didn't know to look at my left eye or that when the bridge of my nose creased, it meant I was holding in tears. Sometimes it wasn't so bad to be with someone who didn't know you that well.

He pumped his fist with fake enthusiasm. "Ready for the bonding to begin?"

I forced myself to smile. "Maybe it'll be better than you think."

He raised an eyebrow. "Or maybe it'll be worse."

And given that beyond him, I saw Jodi approaching us wearing the exact same shirt as me, I felt inclined to agree.

※

The last time I'd gone on the winter retreat was my freshman year. My parents had forced me. Time had stood still out here in Podunk, Missouri, and the dilapidated facilities looked exactly as I remembered. Two small dormitories flanked a sand volleyball court. Beside them stood a large, steel-sided building where we ate meals, held worship services, and played awful, goofy games. The rest of the grounds were open fields surrounding a large pond. It probably looked beautiful in the summer, but with my sour mood and the biting sleet, it appeared desolate.

Jodi and I peeled off from Eli and Connor to follow the rest of the girls to our dorm. We walked in silence in our matching shirts. This justified all the extra dollars I'd once spent to avoid the clearance racks. Every chaperone—even Brian—said, "You girls call each other? Hardy-har-har."

Hilarious.

Each stark bedroom contained a desk and four bunk beds. Jodi and I walked the hallway together. While we weren't on the best of terms, I barely knew the names of the other girls.

I cleared my throat, struggling for the right words to clarify that we'd share a room. "So, do you think we should—"

"Jodi, in here!"

We turned toward the voice. Two juniors—Molly and Lucy—stood in the doorway of a nearby room. Jodi had actually spent time at youth group recently. Of course she knew people.

Both girls seemed to get uncomfortable when they noticed me. Molly tugged at her blonde ponytail. "Hey, Skylar."

"Hey, Molly. Lucy."

Lucy smiled kindly. "There's plenty of room for you too."

"Thanks."

Molly grinned at our shirts. "Did you two plan to—"

"No," I interrupted.

"I like your earrings," Jodi said, leaning closer to Molly for a better look. "Did your boyfriend get you those?"

She blushed. "Yeah, for Valentine's Day."

"Lucky girl."

With disgust, I tossed my sleeping bag and duffle onto a thin mattress. Was it any wonder that everyone at church hated me but loved Jodi?

"Abbie didn't come?" Lucy asked.

It touched me that she asked, that someone besides Connor and Chris noticed she wasn't here. I hoped my smile conveyed this. "I think she felt kind of weird."

"Are you changing?" Jodi asked as I pulled a shirt from my bag.

I motioned to our clothes. "I'd rather not walk around like this the rest of the night."

Jodi rolled her eyes. "Always have to stand out, don't you?"

I yanked the chocolate-colored shirt over my head and gave her a wry smile. "Yeah, brown shirt and jeans. I'll be a real show stopper."

Molly and Lucy watched us with big, round eyes. I really didn't want to fight in front of them. I left.

"What's her problem?" I heard Molly ask, but the main door slammed shut before I heard Jodi's response. I imagined she had a whole list of things to share.

The only place to go was the auditorium. I found Eli already there, oddly the one person who probably felt more out of place than me. He smiled, and his cheeks reddened a touch, as if embarrassed to be caught by himself. I'd always thought Eli looked cutest like this, rather than with his usual cocky demeanor.

"I guess we're supposed to be in here . . ." He glanced about the vacant room. So typical—without the group, he floundered.

I shrugged. "It seems like that's what we did freshman year. I can't really remember."

"The only thing I remember from that retreat was following you all over the place." His blush deepened. Wow, he was cute. "I'm pretty sure you're the only reason I came."

I averted my eyes and walked along the strange particle-board wall. I hoped he couldn't tell how flattered I felt.

"So." Eli stuffed his hands deep in his pockets and shuffled alongside me. "How are you and Connor doing?"

I didn't really want to go into it with him. "Fine."

He shook his head. "You're a better person than I am. I couldn't put up with them for another second."

"Them?" I made myself take a deep, calming breath. "Jodi and Connor?"

"Yeah." He chuckled, but not like he thought it was funny. "What's her deal, anyway? It's like, make up your mind. When she was with him, she was into me. She gets me, and then she's into him again. Crazy, right?"

"Crazy," I murmured.

A gaggle of giggling freshman girls entered on the other side of the room. They seemed so young. How strange to think Abbie had been close to their age when she got pregnant.

Eli glanced at them for only a second before returning his attention to me. "I don't know how you're putting up with it. You must really love Connor to let him get away with all that."

I mulled this over. Letting Connor get away with all of what? As far as Eli knew, all I had supposedly put up with was Connor giving Jodi a safe ride home. Unless Lisa had blabbed about Connor keeping it a secret.

Or maybe there was more to the story.

"So Jodi talks to you about Connor?" I said with a smirk. I hoped to appear amused rather than hungry for information.

"Not willingly, but I really got in her face about this one. I mean, it's just sick. Pretending to be drunk so he'd come get her?"

I tried to keep my cool but couldn't help it. "She only pretended?"

Eli let out a low whistle. "Guess Connor doesn't know either. What a shock that'll be."

"But Lisa said you were off with some other girl when Jodi left. How do you know for sure she wasn't drunk?"

"Lisa said that?" Eli rolled his eyes. "How drunk was *she*? I went to the bathroom. I was gone about five minutes, and when I came back, Jodi'd already left. Unless she really slammed 'em down, I doubt she was even buzzed when she left."

My mind whirled with this information. She'd planned it. How could Connor be so stupid to not even notice? But even as I thought it, I knew it wasn't fair. Jodi had mastered the art of deception years ago.

"I can't believe she admitted it to you," I said.

"Well, I really got in her face. It's obvious she's doing all this to get back at you. I feel kinda responsible."

At some point I'd leaned closer to him. I didn't know when it had happened, but now I had to tilt my head back pretty far to look into his eyes. "You shouldn't feel responsible. You're not the one doing all the pretending."

His mouth curled into a humorless smile. "Bet that changes everything. I mean, if she'd been drunk when she kissed him—"

"She kissed him?" So much for cool and collected.

Eli blinked rapidly. "I thought you knew."

I spotted Connor and Chris entering across the room. "No," I said through gritted teeth. "He left that out."

23

"Skylar?" Connor called as I fled through the other set of doors. "Skylar, wait up!"

I marched down the slippery hill, toward the pond. I'd been stupid enough to leave my jacket in the dorm room, although right then my anger kept me plenty warm.

Connor finally caught up. "What'd he say to you?" He grabbed my elbow and made me stand there with him. "What'd he say?"

"Nothing of interest, really. He just filled me in on a few tidbits you left out when you told me about that ride home." The sleet had turned into damp snow. It stuck to our hair and eyelashes and lined the bare trees. A perfect backdrop for a romantic moment.

"I don't know exactly what he said, Skylar, but it's not like it sounds."

"You kissed her!"

"I . . ." Connor faltered. "*She* kissed *me*."

I put on a smile. "Ohhh. *She* kissed *you*. Well, that's much better." I stalked away as best I could on the slick grass.

"Skylar, wait." Connor trotted alongside me.

I glared at him. "Get real, Connor. You guys kissed and you didn't tell me."

"I know, I—"

"You said you *just* drove her home."

"That's true. What—"

"How's that true? You guys kissed. That's a lot more than 'just' a drive home. Don't you think?"

"Skylar, please don't—"

"What happened to your rules about getting all the cards out on the table? About talking to each other about things?" I shook my head, furious with myself. "I should've known there was more to the story when you didn't tell me yourself."

"Skylar, if you'd listen for just a second—"

"No!" I yanked away as he tried to touch me. "You've had almost a whole week to tell me, to talk to me, and I had to hear about this from Eli. Why don't you just admit that you like her?"

"I *don't* like her. I told you that," Connor said through a clenched jaw.

I squeezed my eyes shut, holding in tears. "You don't want to like her, but you do. Otherwise you'd have told me about giving her a ride, about kissing her—"

"She started to kiss me, but I pushed her away before anything happened," Connor snapped. "I don't cheat."

"You know, it doesn't even matter," I said, looking away from him, into the wind so he couldn't tell I was crying. "We've already broken up."

"We don't need to break up. That's not going to fix anything."

"Nothing in this is fixable. There's no winding back the clock to last Saturday."

"That isn't the real problem and you know it."

I laughed. "Well, I don't know what you're talking about, because that's *exactly* the problem."

Connor gave me a hard look. "What about how you're suddenly going into nursing? What about these weird clothes you've got on?"

I folded my arms over my chest. "There's nothing wrong with what I'm wearing. Or with nursing."

"It's not you," Connor said. "You're trying to be someone you're not."

"Whatever. You're the one stupid enough to fall for Jodi just because she's throwing herself at you, so I don't want to hear it."

Connor's gaze roamed my face as if searching. For what? "I still think we can make it, Skylar. But we both have to want it."

I turned to the pond. I didn't want him seeing how badly I wanted it. "I went through this Jodi thing with Eli. I'm not doing it again."

"I'm not going to do that to you." His hands warmed my back. I wanted to let go, to fall against him. I remained rigid. "Doesn't it mean anything that I love you?"

"Eli said he loved me. My dad vowed in front of everyone, including God, that he'd love my mom forever, and look what happened."

"So I'm being punished for the actions of the other guys in your life?"

"She kissed you, and you didn't tell me," I said in a quiet voice. "What am I supposed to think?"

"That I'm an idiot." Connor took my hands in his. "Maybe you're right, okay? Maybe Jodi was after me this whole time, maybe she did just want to break us up. But when I told you all I did was give her a ride home, it's because to me that's all it was. I don't want to be with her, I want to be with you."

If he hadn't said the word *maybe* about fifty times in his speech, *maybe* I'd have been tempted.

The jingling of my cell phone kept me from having to respond. "The baby," I said as I reached for my back pocket. "Hello?"

"We're leaving for the hospital," Dad said.

My heart raced. This was it. "How long have her contractions been going?"

"She's having them every ten minutes."

Ugh. This wasn't it. "She needs to be having them every four. The book says every four minutes, a minute long, for an hour."

"Your sister says it's time. I'm sure she knows better than the book."

"Abbie also said it was time a week ago. Do you see a baby?"

In the background, I heard Abbie whining, "Let's go. Let's go now."

"Can you meet us there?" Dad asked, sounding out of breath.

"She needs to be having them every four minutes. Every *four* minutes." Connor reached for my hand, but I brushed him away.

"We're going to the hospital," Dad said in a firm voice. "If it's false labor, they'll just tell us to turn around."

"Dad—"

"Do you have a ride back?"

I thought of the Rosses' van and looked at Connor. He must have heard my dad because he nodded. "Connor can bring me."

Again, I heard Abbie. "Let's go *now*."

"Hurry, Skylar," Dad said, then the line went dead.

I closed my phone, heart still racing. "They're taking her to the hospital."

"Go get your stuff. I'll tell everyone what's going on. We'll meet at the car."

"It's probably pointless." I ran my fingers through my wet, icy hair. "The doctor said it could still be weeks. They need to distract her."

His hands warmed my shoulders. "You need to be there for your sister even if this isn't the real thing. Now hurry. We're leaving as soon as possible."

If Connor hadn't yanked me the whole way back, I probably never would've moved. Even the slight possibility of this being it, not just Abbie overreacting, paralyzed me. A baby. A baby girl. Abbie's baby girl.

We were about to meet her.

The room darkened as someone loitered in the doorway. "Connor said Abbie's getting ready to have the baby."

I rerolled my unused sleeping bag. "Yeah, I'm sure you were the first person he told. Now that I'm out of the picture."

Jodi swallowed. "Skylar—"

I halted her with a hand. "I just want to know what's wrong with you that you can't leave my boyfriend alone. Is this about getting back at me? Is this still about Eli?"

She sank onto the bottom bunk across the room, onto Molly's coat. "In the beginning it was. I just thought it'd be kind of funny to mess with you. But now . . ." Jodi wrung her hands. "I really do care about him, Skylar."

"That's nice." I threw my bag onto my shoulder. "Now if you'll excuse me—"

"I felt guilty."

Those words stopped me in my tracks. She continued speaking even though I didn't face her.

"I can't remember ever feeling guilty before." She took a deep breath. "I want you to know I'm not gonna go after Connor anymore, okay? This weird vendetta thing between us—it's over."

I turned to her. "I'd have to be an idiot to believe you," I said. "And you can have him."

She didn't say anything else as I left the room.

Connor already had the van idling. When I rolled open the side door to toss in my stuff, I jumped at the sight of Chris.

"You're coming too?"

He nodded.

"This is stupid. She's not even having the baby. It's too soon."

"Just get in," Connor said.

I opened the passenger door but stared at him. "Let me drive. You guys stay here."

"We're coming with you." He released the parking brake. "Get in and buckle up."

"I don't want you coming with me. Stay. Be with Jodi."

Connor glared at me. "Don't turn this into something it's not."

"Skylar, get in the car," Chris pleaded. He seemed so panicked about getting back in time, I didn't think twice about doing what he asked.

"So words *do* occasionally mean something to you," Connor said as he put the van in reverse. "Just not words that *I* say."

I plastered a sweet smile on my face. "Did you know Jodi wasn't actually drunk the other night?"

His mouth pressed into a line. "What are you talking about?"

"She did the whole weepy, confessional bit, didn't she? I can't believe you fell for her drunk-girl routine. It's, like, one of her oldest tricks."

Chris leaned between us. "Do I want to know what's going on?"

"No," Connor snapped. "Skylar, put on your seat belt."

"When Jodi's actually drunk, she gets all high-pitched and giggly. Just a little tip for the future."

"Okay, fine." Connor turned onto the surprisingly dry road. "Be unsafe. I don't care."

I waited until Connor accelerated onto the interstate before quietly fastening my seat belt. I wouldn't be much good to Abbie if I was dead.

"Thank you," Connor said.

It made me want to unbuckle it. Which made me realize how little I'd changed.

❀

We walked up the ramp of Shawnee Mission Hospital's maternity ward as Mom, Dad, and Abbie walked down.

"What happened?" Chris asked before I could say anything snarky.

"False labor," Mom said.

I smiled wryly at Dad. "Hmm. Really."

217

He just shrugged.

"Sorry to make you all drive out here for nothing." Abbie frowned at me. "I'm barely even dilated."

"No worries," I said. "I'd had enough of the retreat anyway."

"You couldn't have been there more than an hour."

"Well, you know Skylar," Connor jumped in. "Quick to judge."

I cocked my head. "Just being honest about what happened. Do I need to explain that concept to you?"

Abbie gave Chris a questioning look, and he shrugged. My parents seemed clueless, as always.

"You guys should get back," Mom said. "You don't want to miss anything."

"I'm not going back. I just need to get my things out of the van." I turned to walk back to the parking spot before either of my parents could argue.

Connor fell into step with me. "There's no reason why the whole weekend has to be ruined. *Or* the whole relationship."

I said it because I wanted to say something shocking. Something that might throw him off like I'd been thrown off. "I'm going to Hawaii with Mom."

"You're what?" He grabbed my arm and tried to keep me there with him, but I pulled away and kept walking. He jogged after me. "Skylar, that's crazy."

"I was mostly staying for you." And suddenly—with the bitterly cold wind and my frozen fingertips—it made so much sense to go. "Who in their right mind would turn down time in Hawaii?"

"What about Abbie?"

"She can come too."

"She decided to stay. *You* helped talk her into it."

"I'm tired of arranging my life around other people. What's so wrong about me spending a summer in Hawaii with my mother? Or maybe I'll go to college there too. My options are pretty open now."

We'd reached the van. Connor turned to me. "You know if you go, it really will be the end of us."

I thought of that black-and-white bathing suit. Of starting a new adventure. Of meeting all new people. Of creating a new life for myself. It would be the same thing I'd be doing if I went away to college. Leaving behind high school and moving on to my real life. The only reason it had gotten complicated was Connor. And surely it couldn't be too hard to leave behind Connor Ross. To let him fade into someone who had helped me onto the right path, who had meant a lot.

Key word: had.

"Please don't do it, Skylar," Connor said, his voice quiet but strong.

I steeled myself. "I can't forgive what you let happen Saturday night."

I expected another round of begging, pleading, and rationalizing. Instead, Connor nodded. He opened the car, handed me my stuff, and moved toward the driver's seat. "Want a ride back to the entrance?"

I shook my head. "I'll walk."

By the time I met up with my family, he and Chris had left.

24

Lucky for me, Abbie had a closet full of distractions.

Nobody in my family appeared to notice how I holed up in my room all weekend. In fact, each of us seemed intent on isolating ourselves. Abbie to Baby No-Name's room, waiting and arranging. Dad to his office to do office stuff. Mom to her closet, where she threw out winter clothes, even though another six to eight weeks of cold weather lay ahead.

I hibernated in my room with my sewing machine, a stack of Abbie's clothes, and her permission to do whatever I liked. I changed out buttons. I ripped out linings. I threw away that polo.

Then, surveying my handiwork, I wept and wept.

Why had God made me so good at things that didn't matter? When it came to important stuff—relationships, expressing feelings—I always blew it.

❋

My sister's voice reached me in my deep, dreamless sleep. "Skylar—the baby."

I opened my eyes to the sight of Abbie holding her stomach, her eyes large saucers. She grabbed my hand

and pressed it to her belly—rock hard. She drew several ragged breaths, and finally her stomach relaxed.

"This is it," she said. "Every five-ish minutes for the last half hour."

"We're supposed to wait an hour."

She looked me in the eyes. "Take me to the hospital."

I resisted until the next contraction came on—three-and-a-half minutes later—and Abbie's face scrunched in pain. I pulled on jeans, grabbed our bag from under the bed, and steadied Abbie as we navigated the dark hall.

I rapped on Mom and Dad's closed bedroom door. "Mom, it's time."

"What?" she asked, her voice sleepy and muffled.

I nudged open the door. "Abbie's in labor."

The covers rustled. "Be right there."

Abbie and I made it down the stairs in time for another contraction. Again, three-and-a-half minutes. "Take me. To. The hospital," Abbie said through labored breaths.

I'd never been so scared.

"Daddy." I touched his sleeping figure on the couch. "The baby's coming."

His feet hit the floor before I finished my sentence. "The seat's in my car. Let's take it."

By the time Abbie's next contraction came, we'd hit the road. Dad drove while Mom and I encouraged Abbie through each pain.

"They really hurt now," Abbie whimpered to Mom. "Those ones I had early in the week . . . I kinda hoped that's as bad as it'd get."

Mom smoothed Abbie's coppery hair. "But just wait until you get your first glimpse of that baby. You won't feel a thing but love." With her free hand, Mom found my leg and patted it.

As I pondered how long it had been since she'd made such a warm gesture, she blew my mind by turning and smiling at Dad in the rearview mirror. "Remember, Paul, when Skylar was born?" She turned back to me, the grin still warming her face. "We were both so stunned we could hardly speak. And I had pushed you for hours and hours. It was excruciating. I remember thinking, 'Why couldn't Adam have picked the fruit?' because I'd never felt pain like that. I—"

"Mom." I nodded at Abbie, whose jaw had flapped open.

"But *you* . . ." She resumed smoothing Abbie's hair. "Three pushes and you popped out."

Abbie smiled, but she looked ghostlike under the glow of streetlights. I wanted to tell her she'd do great, that I was so proud of her, but another contraction started. Not long after it ended, we arrived at the hospital.

"When can I get the epidural?" Abbie asked as the delivery nurse fussed with her IV. Abbie's face glistened with sweat from her last few contractions.

"I'll put a call in to the anesthesiologist. First you need this bag of fluids in you."

Abbie frowned up at the IV pole. "How long will that take?"

"Twenty or so minutes."

My sister's head flopped onto the pillow, and she released a groan.

"That's not too bad," I attempted. "Just a couple more contractions."

She glared at me.

The nurse's gaze clicked over each member of the family. "Will you all be in here for delivery?"

"No," Dad said. "We'll be in the—"

"Stay," Abbie whimpered. With one hand she reached for Mom, and with the other, Dad. "Please, I want you all in here." She looked at the nurse. "Is that okay?"

She shrugged. "It's your baby."

Abbie blanched.

"I'll have the anesthesiologist come talk to you." With a smart turn on her heel, the nurse turned to leave.

In a couple years, that could be me. I bet working in labor and delivery was a lot of fun. Greeting all the new faces as they popped into the world.

I evaluated the nurse's outfit as she closed the door to Abbie's room. The work must be rewarding, or no one would put up with those ugly white shoes and weird geometric-print outfits.

Abbie crunched into an ice cube. "I should've done birthing classes." She looked at me. "Why didn't I listen to you?"

Mom perched on the edge of Abbie's bed and brushed her bangs from her face. "The nurses will tell you what to do. Don't worry."

"Do people still die in childbirth?" Panic filled Abbie's face. "What if something—"

And then another contraction came, stealing her focus. We stood around her bed, silent as she grimaced in pain. I glanced at Mom and Dad and found their attention locked on Abbie. They certainly hadn't made this last year easy on us, but at least now when it really counted, they could rally around her.

Two contractions later, the anesthesiologist, a strong-looking man in his thirties, rolled a cart into the room. "Abigail Hoyt? I hear you've expressed interest in an epidural."

My sister smiled, exhausted. "Whatever you've got."

He didn't show any surprise at my sister's age, just laughed, loud and friendly. "Well, I'm Dan, and since we have a few minutes while we wait on those fluids"—he jabbed at the half-full baggie—"let me go ahead and explain how an epidural works."

"Abbie's getting low on ice water." Dad grabbed her cup from the bedside table. "I'll be right back."

"Skylar, why don't you text the Rosses that the baby's on its way?" Mom motioned to her purse. "I'm sure they'd want to know."

I glanced at the clock. "At 2:30 in the morning?"

"Amy doesn't keep her cell phone on overnight. This way she'll know as soon as she wakes up and turns it on."

I ventured to the small, hard couch and texted Amy. After a minute's thought, I sent a text to Chris as well. He likely didn't turn his phone off these days, but I doubted he'd mind the interruption.

As I finished, I overheard Abbie saying, "My sister's going into nursing."

I looked up and found her chatting with the delivery nurse, who smiled at me. "Good for you. Do you know what you want to specialize in?"

I shrugged. "My friend's a postpartum nurse. Oh, maybe you know her. She works here. Heather Silver?"

The nurse's smile widened even more. "Oh, Heather's wonderful. She—"

"There's another one coming." Abbie leaned forward, fingers spread across her stomach. "Ow, ow, ow."

"You're doing great, Abbie," the nurse said in a calm voice. She evaluated the ever-important baggie of fluids. "And not much longer until the epidural."

Abbie whimpered.

Dan, who'd stepped to the side where he fussed with vials and paperwork, said to me in a hushed voice, "Will you help me with your sister when the time comes? She needs someone calming and familiar to focus her while I insert the needle."

"Sure." I hoped I sounded calm and confident, like I would as a nurse. "What do I do?"

"Well, I'll have Abbie sit on the edge of the bed with a pillow in her lap. Then she'll bend forward so I can get a clean angle on her spine—"

"Her spine?" A wave of nausea rippled through me. "Like in her back? *That* spine?"

"That's the one." His eyes crinkled when he smiled, same as Eli. "I promise your sister will be just fine. I do this all the time."

Abbie collapsed back on the bed as the contraction ended, her face red like she'd just run a mile. "I can't handle another one of those things."

The nurse smiled as she studied something on Abbie's monitor. "Probably just one more and then you can have the epidural."

"And I won't feel the contractions?" Abbie asked between huffs and puffs.

225

"When we get real close, you'll be able to tell you're having them, but it'll be nothing like this." Something flashed on Abbie's screen, and the nurse leaned closer. "I need to go check on another girl, but I'll be right back."

"Mommy." Abbie reached for Mom's hand. "I can't go to Hawaii with you."

"Shh." Mom patted Abbie. "You just focus on having that baby girl. We'll talk about it later."

"I want us to be together. Everyone. We should be a family." Giant tears rolled down Abbie's cheeks.

I glanced at Dan. He appeared too busy with all his gadgets to pay any attention to the unfolding family drama. I bet he heard lots of weird stuff, being a part of all these intimate moments.

"Abbie, we'll always be a family." Mom looked at Dad as he entered the room, ice water in hand. "Nothing can change that."

Okay, was I crazy, or had I heard a tiny bit of hope in her voice? Maybe our family wasn't lost. Maybe Mom could find a way to get over what Dad did all those years ago.

And if Mom could forgive and the two of them found a way to be happily married, maybe it wasn't too late for Connor and me either.

Ten minutes and two contractions later, the nurse returned. "Abbie, it's the time you've been waiting for." She pulled the drained bag of fluids off the IV pole.

Abbie croaked a meager cheer.

Dan rolled his cart to Abbie's bedside. "Okay, Abbie. Remember how I showed you?" As Abbie grabbed her pillow, he motioned to me. "Skylar, my RN-in-training, ready to come help?"

I nodded, suddenly unable to speak, and shuffled toward the bed. That seasick feeling returned—same as I always felt the first day on a cruise—and my mouth felt gauzy.

"You okay?" Dad asked.

"I don't know why there'd be anything wrong with you." Abbie curled her body over the pillow. "I'm the one getting a needle jammed in my spine."

As she said it, the needle glinted in the light. It was long. Oh so long. And the idea of where Dan would stick . . .

My stomach pitched again. I tried to blink away the black dots, tried to crouch in front of my sister and be supportive.

"Grab her!" Mom screamed.

My eyes closed, and somewhere in the distance, something crashed.

25

My head ached, and I could hear a lot of fussing. Was the baby coming? Had I missed it?

"Are you okay?" Dad's voice cut through the fog.

I cracked open my eyes to see Mom and Dad crouched in front of me, panic lining their faces. Behind them, Abbie sat curled on the bed. Dreamy Dan stood next to her.

"Did I miss it?" I asked, sounding like a feeble old lady.

"Skylar, you hit the floor about fifteen seconds ago," Dad said as he helped me to my feet.

"How about if you take Skylar out of the room, sir?" Dan said. "I'd like to get Abbie taken care of before the next contraction comes." He raised his eyebrows at Mom. "You okay to stay?"

I touched the end of Abbie's bed because I couldn't reach her. "Sorry."

She grinned at me. "Always trying to steal my show, huh?"

I managed a weak smile and let Dad lead me out the door.

"I can't believe that happened. I just kept looking at that big needle and—" I shuddered.

"Not a fan myself." Dad smiled kindly. "We'll take in

some fresh air while they get Abbie situated. Then we'll come back."

The freezing midnight air did just the trick. We strolled along the sidewalk, the moonlight bright on our faces.

"I can't believe my baby girl is about to have a baby girl," Dad said. In a husky voice he added, "I wanted so much more for her."

I'd never heard Dad say anything even slightly negative about the baby. Mom had been all doom and gloom. Dad seemed to have taken on the task of balancing her out.

I didn't know how to answer him. Of course we wouldn't have wished this for Abbie, yet if the nurse had walked out right then and told us it had been a mistake—that Abbie wasn't really pregnant—we'd all be disappointed. We'd all feel like a death had occurred. Regardless of the circumstances, we wanted this baby.

"What do you think life will be like for her?" I asked.

"Her, the baby, or her, Abbie?"

"Abbie."

Dad frowned. "I think it largely depends on her. Even though your mom and I had each other, it was still so overwhelming at times. And we were so immature. We'd both been raised by Christian families, but we were early in our own journeys of faith."

He rested a hand on my shoulder, Dad-style. "As a kid, I thought God made rules just to have them. Just to make our lives difficult and suck the fun out of everything. But as I've aged, I've come to see that God's way makes so much sense. Think of all the problems in our lives, in our world, that exist because of sex happening outside of the marriage relationship. Diseases, abortions . . ." He swallowed. "Divorces." He squeezed me. "But no matter the circumstances, a new baby is something to be celebrated. Your mother and I felt that with you, and we feel it about the little one coming tonight."

I leaned against him. I loved my dad.

"It'll be a tough, lonely road for your sister. Especially if she goes to Hawaii."

I swallowed. "I don't think Abbie's going."

Dad blinked at me. "She told you that?"

"Chris Ross kinda talked her out of it." I kicked at a stray bit of gravel. "But the thing is, recently I've been feeling like I want to go."

Dad didn't show any emotion right away. Or maybe I just couldn't see it because we were between streetlamps. "Is that so?"

"Yeah." I didn't want to tell my dad about the dreams, about the bathing suit. Those weren't the kinds of things he understood. "I just need to be away from here for a little bit. I don't want to go permanently. Maybe just for the summer, then come back here for school."

Dad didn't say anything.

I couldn't stand it any longer. "Are you mad?"

He turned to me, his forehead wrinkled. "No."

"Disappointed?"

Now a smile tugged at the corners of his mouth. "Honey, you're eighteen. While I've never looked forward to your moving out of the house, that time's approaching. Even if you do all your schooling here in the city, I imagine you'll get your own place before too long." He ruffled my hair. "I trust you to do what's best for you. To do what God's asking."

I leaned against him again. "Thanks, Daddy."

We'd circled the maternity wing and reached the main entrance. Dad looked toward the doors. "How you feeling? Better?"

I touched the bump on the side of my head and winced. "I'm still in some pain, but I guess I shouldn't complain to Abbie, huh?"

Dad chuckled as we started up the ramp. "Probably not." The doors into the waiting room glided open. "Have you talked to Connor about the Hawaii thing?"

I opened my mouth to respond when I spotted him. "Connor."

He and Chris turned to look at us. They both wore baseball hats and wrinkled clothes they'd obviously grabbed off the floor.

"How is she?" Chris asked as Connor said, "What happened to your head?"

I touched my forehead. "I apparently don't do well with needles."

"She's fine," Dad answered Chris.

I forced my gaze away from Connor and smiled at Chris. "She's doing great. They just gave her the epidural."

"What happened?" Connor asked.

"Oh, it's totally normal," Dad said. "It's just a procedure to deaden Abbie's nerves so she doesn't feel the pain."

Connor reddened. "I, um, I actually meant Skylar's head."

"Oh." I blushed as well. "I was supposed to help keep Abbie calm during the epidural, but I saw the needle and sorta fainted instead."

Chris bit his lower lip. "It was that bad?"

231

"Are you okay?" Connor's fingertips hovered around my bump, like he wanted to touch me but couldn't bring himself to.

"Dad took me outside for a walk." I glanced at the double doors leading into the ward. "We should get back there, but . . ." I stared at Connor. I wanted to say something to make everything go back to the way it had been those first few weeks. When everything was new and perfect.

Connor lowered his hand without touching me. "We'll be here."

"We'll keep you updated," Dad said.

He nodded at the receptionist, and she buzzed us into the wing. As the door swung closed, my gaze never strayed from Connor's face, and his never left mine. I hoped it meant he felt as willing to forgive as I did.

Childbirth, though miraculous, also turned out to be disgusting.

I kinda suspected it from TV, but it was different to be in there. To hear Abbie crying, and to see . . . well, stuff. I'll leave it at that.

"I can't do it anymore." Abbie collapsed onto her pillow, face sweaty and tomato red. Dad dabbed her with a cloth.

"Good job, Abbie," Mom said.

"You're doing great." It seemed like the millionth time I'd said it. There were only so many words available to encourage a girl in labor. I sometimes peppered in "not much longer," although that felt less and less true. Even to me.

Dr. Ridgway had been surveying Abbie's monitor. "Alright, Abbie," she said, her voice somehow both warm and commanding. "We've got another contraction coming. Get ready to push."

Abbie whimpered.

I glanced at the clock. She'd been pushing for thirty minutes, but it seemed longer. I could only imagine how she felt.

"Deep breath," Dr. Ridgway said, "and push!"

We dove into the routine we'd perfected over the last half hour—Dad supported Abbie's back, Mom and I each took a leg, and all three of us said over and over, "Good job, Abbie. You're doing great. Almost there."

"Another breath," Dr. Ridgway instructed.

Abbie rested long enough to gather another lungful of air, then struggled back up.

"Come on, Abbie," we chanted. "You're doing great. Push. Push."

"Great job, Abbie," Dr. Ridgway said. "And one more breath before the big, baby-moving push."

Abbie collapsed and seemed unwilling to resume pushing.

"You can do it, honey," I heard Dad whispering as he struggled to prop her up.

Dr. Ridgway turned on her motivational voice. "This is the baby-moving push, Abbie. You're almost there."

"You can do it, Abbie," I said.

Her face turned so red, I forgot to cheer her on until Dr. Ridgway cried, "The head's out!"

Abbie went limp on the bed. "All that work for just the head?"

"You're doing great. The head's the worst part of it," Mom said.

233

"That's right," Dr. Ridgway said. "Just one more set of pushes, Abbie, and you'll have this baby. And here comes the next contraction. Deep breath, and up. Push, push, push!"

"Push, push, push!" we yelled.

And barely a minute later, a new sound entered the delivery room—a loud, squawky cry. Out the baby came, all red and mucusy and perfect. My breath caught, and we all stopped and stared.

"Congratulations." Dr. Ridgway beamed at Abbie and turned the newborn where she could see. "You have a beautiful baby boy."

26

As dawn broke on Monday, March 2, Connor and I sat side by side in Abbie's recovery room.

"A boy," Connor whispered, his voice full of awe.

We all kept saying it, marveling. How strange to expect one thing with such certainty but then get the opposite.

I smiled as I watched Abbie snuggle Owen Joshua Hoyt. Chris perched on the edge of the bed, stroking Owen's head of soft, dark hair. Mom and Dad had left not long before to shower and pick up breakfast. And, I assumed, to start redoing that pink nursery.

"Did she seem disappointed at all?" Connor asked.

I shook my head. "She had about a dozen girl names she couldn't pick from, but she always had a perfect boy name in mind. I think she was relieved."

"Funny how sometimes God prepares us for things without us even realizing it," Connor said.

For the first time in over a week, I reached for his hand and laced our fingers together. "I'm glad you're here." I smiled, oddly bashful.

Connor smiled as well, but it looked like a struggle. As if he'd commanded the corners of his mouth upward.

And when he pried his fingers out of mine, I knew. It really was over.

"I have to confess something." He glanced at Chris and Abbie, who were absorbed in their own soft conversation. "This probably isn't the best time."

I sighed, my breath wobbling as I held in tears. "It rarely is."

"You were right." Connor's fingers danced about his lap. "I do have feelings for Jodi."

This victory came with no joy. I stared at my still hands.

"But at the same time, I really believe I'm in love with you, that you're the girl I want to be with." He tugged at his collar and shifted in his seat. "Yet I *am* attracted to the idea of helping Jodi, of fixing her. Just like you said." He leaned into his hands, covering his face. "I don't know what's wrong with me."

I sat there stiff and achy. What did he expect me to do now?

"What do you expect me to do now?" I asked. Hey, that had been pretty easy—articulating what I meant. Maybe there was hope for me after all.

Connor shook his head, which was still buried in his hands. "I don't know." He leaned back and looked at me, eyes big and sincere. He had beautiful eyes. I'd always thought so. "I think you were right to suggest time apart. I need to work out this . . ." He waved his hand, unable to come up with the word. "This thing I have. This disorder."

My voice barely registered above a whisper. "How long do you think that'll take?"

He shook his head, apparently unable to answer me.

We watched Owen fuss as Abbie passed him to Chris, then he settled back to sleep.

"Jodi committed her life to Christ this weekend," Connor said. "We were sitting out on the volleyball courts. She told me about how she originally started coming to church and flirting with me just to get a rise out of you, but now that we'd broken up, she felt guilty."

"She said something similar to me as I left," I said, voice tight. "You believe her?"

He nodded. "I think God's really gotten ahold of her."

"Time will tell."

"You doubt she's for real?"

"I really don't know anymore."

"I wish you could've been there," Connor said, sounding wistful. "Leading her in that prayer . . . It was awesome. I've never been a part of anything like that."

I swung my legs a little, watching the pendulum of my feet. I didn't know if I wanted an answer to my next question. "So are you, like, gonna date her or something?"

Connor frowned. "I don't think so. I mean, if nothing else, she's leaving for Tennessee in the fall."

That's not what he was supposed to say. He was supposed to say of course he wouldn't, that he loved me and couldn't imagine life apart. That he knew these feelings for Jodi would go away.

"You're obviously free to date whomever you want," Connor said.

"Gee, thanks."

"I didn't mean it like that. All I meant is, I don't expect you to sit around and wait for me to be ready. Who knows how long it could be. Months, or years, or—"

"Why don't we stop talking?" I interrupted, watching my nephew. "It's ruining the moment."

The only other thing Connor said to me was "bye," nearly an hour later when he and Chris left.

I pulled my chair alongside Abbie's bed as she fed Owen.

She smiled at me, glowing yet drowsy. "Crazy, huh? I have a kid."

I relaxed as best as I could in my hard seat, feeling exhaustion settle in. I hadn't even birthed anyone. "You're doing great."

She glanced at my bruised forehead. "How you feeling?"

"I think I'm supposed to be asking you that."

"I didn't collapse on the floor." Abbie giggled, then grimaced. "Didn't know I used that muscle when I laughed."

"Serves you right." I propped my feet on the edge of her bed. "I was just trying to help you."

"Guess that's the end of your nursing career, huh?"

I considered this. "I probably wouldn't make a very good one. Back to square one."

Abbie gave me a look. "C'mon, Skylar. We all know what you're going to be."

"Let's talk about that later," I said.

She propped Owen up to burp, his wobbly head cupped in her hand. Though only seven pounds and eleven ounces, his burp filled the room. We both giggled. Immature, maybe, but of course we were fifteen and eighteen.

"Wanna hold him?" Abbie asked.

I grinned and reached for him. He peered up at me, then his eyes closed as he nestled against me to sleep.

"Who do you think he looks like?" Abbie asked as she tidied her ponytail. "Chris thinks he looks like me."

I ran my finger along Owen's sheer cheek. "I don't know." His face was splotchy and his eyes a strange, colorless gray that the pediatrician promised would change. "Maybe if we had baby pictures of you and Lance, we could tell."

Her expression changed, and I regretted mentioning Lance. "How could he not want Owen?" Abbie reached for her son, stroking his mass of hair. "I mean, I'm terrified, but I couldn't give up knowing him."

"Maybe Lance will change his mind."

Owen mewed and stretched but didn't open his eyes.

"Should he be allowed?" Abbie asked. "It's not like I'll be given breaks."

"I think the decision's yours," I said. "You felt God calling you to raise Owen. He didn't bring you this far just to abandon you."

Abbie kissed Owen's head before nestling into her pillow. "You're right. He'll watch out for us." She smiled at me. "And for you."

As Abbie's soft breathing turned to snoring, I thought about everything God had brought us through in the last nine months. No, he wouldn't abandon us now.

When Mom and Dad returned, they had bagels and juice for both of us.

"How's our little guy doing?" Mom asked, stealing Owen from me. "I'm afraid I'll be worthless to you, Abbie. I don't know a thing about little boys."

Dad dropped a kiss on Abbie's head. "Feeling okay?"

She nodded. "They brought me some meds. Peeing is still kind of an adventure—"

"Oh, Abigail, don't talk like that." Mom's face puckered. "I don't like that word."

Dad smiled. "Peeing?"

Mom attempted a cross look but couldn't seem to erase her smile. "Don't you start too." Her voice lilted playfully.

Abbie and I glanced at each other. It was like spotting a deer in a field. It looked so beautiful, you wanted to call everyone's attention to it, but of course that could startle it away.

Abbie apparently decided to risk it. "You two are in a good mood," she said innocently with a sip of her juice.

Mom and Dad exchanged a look, as if deciding who should address this. Dad finally said, "We've decided to return to counseling."

I grinned, and Abbie, in her emotional state, burst into tears.

Funny how even with everything I'd just lost, the restoration of my family still made it feel like the perfect day.

27

Jodi thought it would do us good to "have a little chat," as she said on my voice mail.

I disagreed, which is why I dodged her calls that first week of Owen's life.

When I returned to school the Monday after he'd been born, avoiding her became impossible, seeing as her locker was next to mine. I found all six of them standing there— Eli, John, Lisa, Alexis, Jodi, and Connor. No one seemed eager to speak.

"Hey, guys," I said, making my way to my locker.

"Hey," they chorused back.

And that took care of everything I had to say to any of them.

Jodi leaned against her locker as I spun in my combination. "How's Owen?"

"Good."

"I called you a couple times."

"I know."

"So, you don't want to talk to me?"

"Basically, no."

She sighed. "I just wanted to tell you I'm sorry. For everything." She glanced over her shoulder at our audience of five. "But I'm kinda glad you didn't take my calls, because now I can apologize in front of all our friends. I'm so sorry for what I did to you."

"Fine." I swapped out books as quick as I could. I didn't need to have this conversation. Especially not with Connor watching. "See ya."

"Wait." Jodi trotted after me, around the corner and away from everyone's watchful eyes. "Skylar, we're, like, sisters in Christ now. We should get along."

"It doesn't work like that." I stopped and faced her. "I don't know what they told you at the retreat, but it doesn't fix everything overnight. Just like me. I thought accepting God's plan for my life would make it easier. Most of the time, it's only made it harder."

Jodi chewed on her lip, mussing her carefully applied lipstick. "Maybe it's because you haven't really accepted his plan."

I blinked at her. "What?"

She gestured to my outfit—a white oxford shirt and dark rinse jeans. "I don't know what this is that you're going through—this weird, plain-clothes phase—but it isn't you. It isn't how God created you."

I rolled my eyes. "Thanks for the tip," I said, then stormed away. Like I needed some girl who'd been a Christian for a week telling me how to live my life.

"You can't expect your life to change just because you sit through Sunday services," Jodi called after me, despite the crowded hallway. "You've got to give it all to him."

❁

"I can't believe I missed so much while I was gone," Heather said as she sorted through the clothing racks. "The baby, you and Connor, your parents."

"It was a wild couple of weeks."

"For you and me both."

Heather had spent the last hour of our shopping trip describing her time in Uganda. Many of the stories were about the patients, but most were about Brent.

She held up several tiny outfits. "I can't decide. I'm getting all of them."

"I know Abbie will appreciate it. Most of what we'd bought had ruffles and bows. Owen wouldn't care now, but he might later."

Heather grinned and tucked the outfits into her basket. "How's Abbie doing?"

I hesitated, thinking of the nervous breakdown I'd witnessed that morning. Overnight, Owen had wanted to eat every ninety minutes. "She doesn't regret keeping him, but . . ."

"It's harder than she anticipated?"

"Yeah."

Heather sighed. "Poor Abbie." She considered the various other baby aisles at Target. "You're sure she doesn't need anything but clothes?"

"Mom and Dad have taken care of everything else. They're so funny. They're redoing the nursery and seem so . . . together." I smiled. "It'd be nauseating if it wasn't such a relief."

"My parents were always real flirtatious." Heather giggled. "I remember once in high school I had friends over, and they saw Mom and Dad all over each other in the kitchen. I was *so* embarrassed. Of course now I know to appreciate that my parents like each other." She glanced around the clothing racks, as if waiting for something else to catch her eye. "You ready to go?"

243

"Almost. I need to grab an extra package of cloth diapers."

My voice must have broadcast my sadness. Heather cocked her head. "What's wrong?"

"Oh, just Connor stuff."

She followed me through the racks of teeny-tiny clothes to the aisles of baby necessities. "So you guys aren't talking at all?"

I shook my head. "He called once, and I asked him not to anymore. He said it was painful not to talk to me, but really it's painful either way."

"Well, it's a breakup." Heather studied me. "You seem like you're doing really well."

Did I? I felt rotten. I shrugged. "I guess I'm okay. Until the first time I run into him out on a date with Jodi, that is."

She gave me a sad smile. "You're around all summer?"

"Looks like it." I sighed. My summer in Hawaii was the one casualty of Mom and Dad's reconciliation. I could probably ask to go stay with Grammy and Papa, but did I really want that? Not with Mom and Dad on the mend. Not with Owen.

So not only would I be stuck at home in the fall while everyone scattered to their selected schools, I wasn't even slated to enjoy my summer break.

"So when do I get to meet Brent?" I asked as we made our way up to the front of the store.

Heather grinned. "Soon. I wanted him to come to church on Sunday, but he's working." She sighed. "I think he might be the one, Skylar."

"You deserve it," I said. That's why I could handle all her

smiling and happiness in the wake of my failed relationship.

"Ooh, look. Swimsuits are in." Heather trotted off toward the colorful racks of bikinis. "Let's go see."

I followed her with a sigh. I didn't need a swimsuit anytime soon. In years past, I'd anxiously awaited the day stores stocked the new suits because spring break always meant a cruise. This year, between Owen's existence and Mom and Dad's counseling bills, I assumed my spring break would be spent watching daytime television and changing diapers.

Heather plunged into the swimsuit displays, full of comments like, "I like this, but not in a halter . . . Ooh, argyle . . . Do they have this in a color other than yellow?"

I opened my mouth to point out the green version when my eye caught on something else. "Look," I said, before realizing it made sense only to me.

Heather looked. "Cute."

I reached to touch it. This wasn't a dream, right? I was really awake? Because it looked exactly like I'd envisioned— black with large white polka dots, thick ties around the neck. And I thought of Connor's words in the hospital: "Funny how sometimes God prepares us for things without us even realizing it."

When I entered my house, baby clothes and the black-and-white swimsuit in the bag dangling from my arm, a wave of concern hit me. I stood there in the doorway trying to put my finger on why. And then I realized.

Someone was baking chocolate chip cookies.

I flinched. "Mom?"

"She's upstairs, honey."

Dad's voice had never sounded so good.

In the kitchen, I found him scraping mismatched lumps of dough onto a cookie sheet. I knew next to nothing about baking, but I did know cookies should be the same size so they baked evenly.

"What are the cookies for?" I asked.

"They're your mom's favorite. I've never made them before." Dad shrugged. "Thought I'd give it a try."

The timer sounded. He pulled out a batch and slid the next sheet in.

I eyed the egg shells on the counter, the mess of measuring cups piled in the sink, the dirty bowl of the rarely used KitchenAid mixer. "You made them from scratch?"

Dad reddened a bit. "Amy Ross gave me her recipe." He placed the cookie sheet where I could see. Some were overdone, and some had hardly baked, but a few looked perfect—golden around the edges, still a little doughy in the middle. He beamed same as when he landed new clients. "Not bad for your old man, huh?"

I forced a smile and took a seat at the bar. "They look great, Dad."

"So, what's wrong?" He scooped one of the cookies off the sheet and dropped it on the counter in front of me.

"Nothing, I'm just . . . tired. I guess Owen's not wild about the crib I picked out."

Dad squinted at me. "I know you a little better than that, honey. You don't look tired, you look depressed. Connor?"

I sighed and broke the cookie in half. "I guess so. He says he just needs some time, but even if he's interested in being my boyfriend again, I don't know that I'm interested in taking him back." I returned the cookie to the counter. I didn't really feel like eating. Especially that rock. "It's just so risky, trusting people. I mean, ultimately he's just going to hurt me again, right?"

Now Dad sighed. "I guess your mom and I are to blame for your cynical view of things." He covered my little hands with his large ones. "There are few things I can guarantee you, Skylar. One is that this won't be the last time someone hurts you. And it's probably not the worst you'll get hurt either."

"Good pep talk."

He smiled. "But love is like a lot of things in life. The people who cost us the most become most dear to us. Look at everything Abbie went through for Owen. Look how needy he is. How he keeps her up at night and wants to be held all the time. And yet Abbie loves him more than anything else in this world."

"I guess."

"And look at Jesus. The pain he went through was so great, yet his love for us is more than we can even comprehend. You see what I'm driving at?"

"No pain, no gain?"

He chuckled. "Something like that."

"But how do you trick yourself into trusting someone after they've hurt you?"

Dad's eyebrows arched. "*Trick* yourself?"

"You know what I mean. How do you trust someone when common sense tells you not to?"

A shadow crossed his face, and I knew he thought of Mom, of how close he came to losing her. Of how he could still lose her. "What it boils down to, I think, is trusting God. Let's use you and Connor as an example. When he comes crawling back to you—and I do mean *when*—you'll have to make the decision of whether or not you want to trust him. But what you're really saying is you trust God will take care of you, even if Connor proves to be untrustworthy. That's what your mother and I are having to learn. To trust that there's nothing too big for God to handle or too big for us to work through as long as he's helping us."

I mulled this over while I took a large bite of my cookie. It was crispy and tasted like I imagined a burned shoe might. With some chocolate. "Dad." I forced myself to swallow. "This is horrible."

He sighed. "I guess I'm no good at cookie making. Business deals, sure. But this clearly isn't my gift."

Abbie entered the kitchen with a swaddled and sleeping Owen. "Mmm, cookies."

"Proceed at your own risk," I said, reaching for my nephew.

"Same to you. He's spitting up like crazy today."

As she transferred him to my arms, Owen arched his back. His face scrunched, and his fists clenched. What a horribly confusing feeling it must be to go from the warm, snuggly comfort he'd always known to this unstable world.

Tears pricked my eyes as I recognized myself in him. My life had felt off-kilter since I woke up from that party on July 15, as if God was in the process of transferring me from one life to another.

"Shh," I whispered to Owen, pulling him close. "You're okay."

In amazement, I watched as his face relaxed and he settled against me. Somehow, despite his discomfort a few seconds before, he was able to trust my security. He didn't seem worried that I'd drop or abandon him, he just drifted back to sleep.

I drew him even closer, hoping to show him he was right to trust.

Acknowledgments

Many thanks to:

My husband, Ben, who reads my books in their primitive form, is a constant source of encouragement, and makes excellent and inspiring chocolate chip cookies.

My Tuesday babysitters, Steve and Beth Hines, and my Thursday babysitters, Ann and Bruce Morrill. I have the best parents and in-laws ever.

My writing friends who read the first draft of this book and offered feedback: Roseanna White, Mary Proctor, Carole Brown, Kasey Heinly, and Colleen Shine Phillips.

Kelli Stouder and Debbie McCool, two of my great encouragers.

Dr. Amy Knapitsch, who answers all my medical questions promptly and kindly.

Cindy Arterburn, whose adoption expertise was invaluable to Abbie's story.

My agent, Kelly Mortimer, who continues to shock me with her love for and belief in Skylar.

And my amazing publishing house, Revell, particularly those I'm in regular contact with—Jennifer Leep, Jessica Miles, Janelle Mahlmann, and Cheryl Van Andel. Thank you for all your hard work.

Stephanie Morrill is a twentysomething living in Overland Park, Kansas, with her high school sweetheart-turned-husband and their young daughter. She loves writing for teenagers because her high school years greatly impacted her adult life. That, and it's an excuse to keep playing her music really, really loud.

Getting a Fresh Start

the reinvention of skylar hoyt

me, just different

STEPHANIE MORRILL

Book 1 in the Reinvention of Skylar Hoyt series

Revell
a division of Baker Publishing Group
www.RevellBooks.com

Is Harder Than It Looks

Book 3 in the Reinvention of Skylar Hoyt series

Available wherever books are sold.

Be the First
to Hear about
Other New Books
from Revell!

Sign up for announcements about
new and upcoming titles at

www.revellbooks.com/signup

Don't miss out on our
great reads!

Revell

a division of Baker Publishing Group
www.RevellBooks.com